Bex Carter 2:

All's Fair in

Love and

Math

All's Fair in Love and Math

Book 2 of the Bex Carter Series

Other books by Tiffany Nicole Smith:

Books 1-5 of the Fairylicious Series

<u>The Bex Carter Series</u>

Book 1: Aunt Jeanie's Revenge

Book 3: Winter Blunderland

Book 4: The Great War of Lincoln Middle (Dec 2013)

This is a work of fiction. Names, characters, places, and incidents are either products of the author's imagination or, if real, are used fictitiously.

ISBN:149430872x

Cover Designed by Littera Designs

Twisted Spice Publications

For everyone who has ever been crushed by a crush.

I'd love to hear from you!

Twitter: @Tigerlilly79

Facebook: https://www.facebook.com/tiffany.smith.735944

Website: authortiffanynicole.com

Email: authortiffanynicole@gmail.com

Bex Carter: 2

All's Fair in Love and Math

Tiffany Nicole Smith

Disclaimer: This is the story of a girl's first crush. It details exactly what NOT to do. You have been warned. ☺

1

Bex + Math = Colossal Fail

facepalm

Aunt Jeanie had to be the best one-eyebrow raiser I knew. I'd tried many times to replicate the look in the mirror, but I could never just raise one eyebrow by itself. Maybe Aunt Jeanie had some special muscle in her forehead or something. Anyway, I cringed as she looked over my report card, giving me the one-eyebrow raise from across the living room. I couldn't blame her. For the most part my grades were okay, but I had gotten a D in math. C's were unacceptable in Aunt Jeanie's house, so I knew she was about to blow a gasket.

"Bex, a D? Really? No one in this house has ever gotten a D. No one in our family has ever gotten a D."

Leave it to me to ruin a family record.

I squirmed on the sofa. I hated disappointing my aunt. "Aunt Jeanie, I'm sorry. But I'm trying my best. I really, really am. The past couple of weeks I've really been starting to understand. I'm sure by the time progress reports come out, I'll have a least a B."

Aunt Jeanie folded my report card and closed her eyes as if she couldn't stand to look at it anymore. "You'd better or you're off the soccer team."

That's what I was most worried about. I loved being on the soccer team, and now I was on probation. I was still on the team, but I only had a few weeks to bring up my grades or I would be kicked off. That would be absolutely tragic. I was the best goalie on the team, and we had a tough season ahead of us.

"Bex, I want you to be successful. Grades come before soccer and anything else. I know you're trying, but try a little harder. Once you fall behind it's hard to catch up."

"Okay, Aunt Jeanie. May I be excused?"

"Yes," she said, handing me my report card. She held it between the tips of her thumb and index finger as if it had cooties. I assumed it wouldn't be going on the fridge with her children's aced spelling tests.

I trudged upstairs to my brand-new bedroom. I felt a little guilty as I entered my beautifully decorated teenage room. Aunt Jeanie had been very nice to finally give me my own space, so I hated to let her down.

After climbing the tiny staircase that led to my bed, I sighed and threw myself onto my soft comforter. I wished bringing up my math grade was as easy as it sounded. The truth was I tried my absolute hardest. I did everything my teacher showed me how to do, but it didn't click. The last concept Mr. Hawthorne had taught finally made sense to me, so hopefully I would start doing better.

My bedroom door was flung open and my little sister entered. "Bex, let's see who won the contest," Ray said.

"What contest?" I asked as she climbed up to my bed as if she'd been invited.

"The contest to see who got the most A's, silly."

I turned my report card over. I was supposed to set a good example for my little sister. I didn't want her knowing I had gotten a D. "Ray, what are you talking about?"

"At school me and my friends had a contest to see who had the most A's," she explained.

"Well, that's fine for your friends, but a contest between us wouldn't be fair. You're in the first grade, and I'm in the eighth . My work is a lot, lot harder than baby work."

"I don't do baby work! First grade is very, very hard. Under the circumstances."

"What?" 'Circumstances' was the word of the week at Ray's school. That meant all week she'd work it into every conversation she had, whether it fit or not.

Reagan went to a fancy private school where Aunt Jeanie also sent her triplets, Priscilla, Penelope, and Francois. We lived with our aunt because our father was in jail and our mother was nowhere to be found. The downside to this was that I truly missed my parents. The upside was that my aunt and uncle were rich and lived in a humongous house. We got to do lots of cool things. The other downside was that Aunt Jeanie and I didn't have the best relationship, but we were working on it.

I took Ray's report card from her. She had all A's and a B in science. She had S's in behavior, which stood for satisfactory. That was good for a kid who had a major behavior problem.

"Ray, this is pretty—"

While I had been paying attention to her report card, she'd snatched mine up from the bed. "Uh-huh. Uh-huh. Uh-huh." Then she gasped. "Bex, you got a D in pre-al-gah-"

I took the report card from her. "That's pre-algebra."

"Oh. Bex, does that mean you're stupid?"

"No, it doesn't mean I'm stupid. This kind of math is really hard. Wait until you get to middle school. What you're doing now is easy as pie."

I longed to go back to my first-grade days of simple addition and word problems that made sense.

"Anyway," Ray said, "I got more A's than you, so I win. What are you going to give me?"

"I'm not giving you anything. I didn't agree to this contest. I told you it wasn't fair."

She folded her arms across her chest and pouted. "But I won. I want my prize!"

I didn't have the patience to deal with one of her monster tantrums. "Fine," I said, climbing down from the bed. I rummaged through my junk drawer. I found a used tube of Chap Stick and an old deflated balloon. "Here you go."

Her face brightened. "Cool! Thanks, Bex!"

Too easy. "You're welcome." I pushed her toward the door. "Now, if you'll excuse me, I need to study."

"Yeah, you do, under the circumstances. Bye!"

Just then the phone rang in the upstairs hallway. I knew it was for me. I answered it and sat against the wall.

"Hey, Austin."

"Hey," he answered. "You sound bummed. What's wrong?"

"Report card day."

"Oh. Enough said. Mine wasn't so hot either."

I sighed. "Mine wasn't that bad. It's only math that's giving me problems. No pun intended."

Austin laughed. "Yeah, math is my worse subject too."

A long awkward pause hung between us. Austin was my friend and had been for a while. I liked him more than a friend and I was pretty sure that he like me more than a friend, but we weren't boyfriend and girlfriend. I wasn't sure why.

"Sooo," I said trying to think of something to say. "Oh, how was your baseball game yesterday."

"It was good. We won. I even scored a homerun."

"That's great," I said. "Maybe I can come to your next game."

"Maybe," Austin said. "That kind of sounds like something a girlfriend would do, doesn't it?"

"Yep. It does." I waited. Was there something he wanted to ask me? I mean, he was the one who mentioned "girlfriend". If he were going to ask, it would have been the perfect time.

"Well, I have to go eat dinner," he said. "I'll talk to you later. Good luck with math."

I sighed again. "Yeah. Thanks." I hung the phone up and trudged back to my bedroom. I wasn't sure what to think. Maybe Austin was just like every other boy and didn't see me as girlfriend material.

After closing the door I sat at my desk. I grabbed my backpack, which was leaning against the chair, and pulled out my heavy pre-algebra book. We were solving two-step linear equations. I had been struggling throughout the entire chapter, but I was finally getting it. Maybe, just maybe, if I stayed focused, I could bring my grade up.

2

Carnivals and Equations

headdesk

For the first time all year, I was actually excited for math class. I couldn't wait to show Mr. Hawthorne how I was finally getting it. Unfortunately, my excitement was short lived.

Mr. Hawthorne must be psychic. Somehow he knew that I had finally gotten a grasp on Chapter 7, because he decided it was time for us to move on to Chapter 8. Really? I'd just caught up and we were moving on.

The day before, Mr. Hawthorne had been like, "Johnny drove 32 miles per hour for 30 minutes and at 48 miles per hour for 45 minutes. How far did he travel?"

It had been hard for me, but I could figure it out. I knew how to get the answer.

But the next day he was all like, "If Johnny drove from point A to point B, how long would it take twenty-five unicorns to eat sixty watermelons, and how many waffles would it take to fill a sink?"

I sank into my seat. Mr. Hawthorne might as well have been speaking alien. Around me the other kids were scribbling away, trying to solve the problem on the board. I didn't even know where to begin.

I dropped my head to my desk, praying that I would miraculously understand this drivel.

"Bex, aren't you even going to try?" Mr. Hawthorne asked.

I let out a huge moan.

"I'll help you individually when I'm done teaching the lesson."

This was an everyday occurrence. I felt bad for Mr. Hawthorne. He tried so much to help me, but I was hopeless.

He came by my desk and tried to explain it to me, but I was even more confused when he was done. "Bex, I think I have something that will help you," Mr. Hawthorne said. "I'll call your aunt this afternoon."

Great. My spot on the soccer team was as good as gone.

"Why the long face, Red?" Random Kid yelled at me on my way to the cafeteria. I had no idea who this kid was, but he yelled things at me in the hallway every day. He always called me Red because of my thick mane of curly red hair.

At least the cafeteria was serving pizza. That always cheered me up after a horrible math class. I grabbed my tray and went to sit at the Awesome Possum table with my absolute best friends in the world—Chirpy, Lily-Rose, and Marishca.

"Aww, what's wrong, Bex?" Lily-Rose asked. She had her arm looped around Maverick's. They were officially MavRose and had been voted the third-cutest couple in the eighth grade.

"Math is what's wrong," I whined. "I just don't get it, and once I do understand something, Mr. Hawthorne moves on to something else."

"I told you I would help," Lily-Rose said as she put a pepperoni onto Maverick's tongue. I couldn't help but roll my eyes. The two of them made an adorable couple, but they had this horrible habit of having to feed each other. It totally should be against school rules. I mean, who wants to see that when they're eating?

"No thanks, Lily-Rose. The last time you tried to help, you ended up yelling at me, remember? I can't work under those conditions."

Lily-Rose shrugged. "Suit yourself."

Chirpy and Marishca were also sitting with their boyfriends. Chirpy and Marishca were both cheerleaders, and Ava G., the most horrid girl in school, had declared that cheerleaders should only date basketball players, so that's what they did.

Dating at Lincoln Middle consisted mostly of sitting together at lunch and hanging out at the skating rink, but I always seemed to be the odd man out.

Everyone was paired up except for me, and maybe, just maybe, I was a tiny, tiny bit jealous. That wasn't the only difference between us. My friends were all short and thin, while I was tall and big-boned. I wasn't overweight, I was just not skinny. Lily-Rose was brown-skinned and wore glasses. Chirpy had short brown hair and looked like a tiny bird, hence the name Chirpy (her real name was Beatrice), and Marishca, my Russian friend, had short blond hair. When we walked as a group, I towered over them like a gorilla. It made me self-conscious sometimes, but there really wasn't anything that could be done about it. I couldn't shrink myself, and I couldn't force my friends to grow.

Don't get me wrong, I don't have anything against people having boyfriends. Sometimes I wished Austin went to Lincoln Middle with me.

Santiago, the Hustler, slid his tray next to mine. Santiago was a business man. He always had some money-making scheme going on.

"Hey, Santiago. How's business?" I asked.

"Booming! I rented out my last bodyguard today. I think it's time to recruit some more. What about you, Bex? You can be intimidating."

Santiago ran a bully bodyguard service where he rented out big eighth-graders to kids who were being bullied. His first customer had been our tuxedo-wearing friend, Jeeves, who was nowhere in sight.

"You seen Jeeves?" I asked Santiago.

"Yeah, he's eating lunch with Cara."

"Oh." I had forgotten that he had started going out with her. It seemed as if everyone was pairing off.

"Hey, lovebirds!" Santiago shouted across the table. "We need to come up with a theme for our carnival booth."

The school's annual carnival was coming up. We had signed up to work a booth together, and now we had to come up with an idea to raise money for the Children's Leukemia Foundation. Some kids were selling baked goods or making arts and crafts. Really anything was acceptable, except for kissing booths.

"What about a fortune-telling booth?" Maverick asked.

"None of us can tell fortunes," Marishca said.

Maverick shrugged. "So what? You think any of those people can really tell fortunes?"

"No, no. This is a good idea," Santiago said. "Definitely good R.O.I."

We all looked at him as if he'd turned purple.

He rolled his eyes. "Return on investment, guys. Meaning we won't have to spend a lot of money to make money. Just tell people general things that they want to hear." He moved his hands around as if running them around a crystal ball and turned on a spooky voice. "Oooh, I sense that you are hoping for something. You have a wish you want to come true." Then he laughed. "Who doesn't?"

"Okay, zat sounds good to me," Marishca said, and everyone else agreed. As far as I was concerned, I didn't care too much about what we did. I was worried about bringing up my math grade and staying on the soccer team.

I have to say that Mr. Hawthorne and Aunt Jeanie worked pretty fast, because when I got home from school that day, I was met with a pleasant surprise.

Aunt Jeanie screamed my name before I even had both feet in the door.

"Where are you, Aunt Jeanie?"

"In the kitchen!"

I dropped my backpack on the dining room table, which Aunt Jeanie hated for me to do, and went into the kitchen.

She was busy making something for her silly Silver Rose Society Committee. They had some event coming up that she was stressed out about.

"Yes?"

"Your math teacher called me today. He thinks a tutor would help you out a lot."

"No, Aunt Jeeeeeanie! You want me to spend all day in school and then come home to work with some geek for hours on math? No thanks!"

She pulled some cookie sheets from the cabinet. "Bex, this is not optional. One of the girls at the club has a nephew that tutors. I already called him, and he's coming by later this evening for your first session."

"This evening? You're not even giving me time to prepare. I don't have time for that tonight. I'm having a teleconference with Chirpy, Marishca, and Lily-Rose."

Aunt Jeanie put her hand on her forehead. "Bex, I have to bake three hundred cookies. I don't have time to argue with you about this."

"Aunt Jeanie, why don't you just buy cookies instead of stressing yourself out?" If I had a kazillion dollars like her, that's what I would do.

"I can't do that, Bex. Sylvia is also bringing cookies, and she always makes her own from scratch. Store-bought cookies just aren't going to cut it."

I didn't have time to worry about the ridiculous rivalries she always seemed to have going on with the women in her group. "Whatever," I muttered. "Call me when the nerd gets here."

At around six o'clock that evening the doorbell rang. I had a sick feeling in the pit of my stomach that it was going to be my new tutor. I thought Aunt Jeanie was wasting my time and her money. I was hopeless when it came to math. If a real classroom teacher couldn't get me to understand this stuff, what made her think some high-school kid could?

I stood at the top of the stairs. The triplets were at the door, jumping up to see through the peephole.

"Who is it?" Priscilla asked.

"I can't see," Francois said. "Let me stand on your back."

"No way!" Priscilla shouted.

I pushed the three of them out of the way. "It's for me. Go upstairs."

"Oh," Penelope said. "It's Bex's tutor because she's stuuuupid."

"Get upstairs before I stupid you!" I shouted.

"That doesn't even make sense," Francois scoffed. "You really *are* stupid."

I lunged toward him and the three of them ran screaming up the stairs.

I looked through the peephole and saw something totally unexpected. You know how in movies when a person comes into contact with someone they really like and they see fireworks? Well how come no one told me that actually happens in real life?

The firework-inducing boy rang the doorbell again. I took a deep breath, wishing I had taken a few moments to check myself out in a mirror.

"Bex, get that!" Aunt Jeanie called from the kitchen.

I gulped, twisted the lock, and pulled the door open. The most gorgeous male specimen I had ever seen in my life stood before me.

"Hello. I'm here to see a Rebecca Carter."

"That's me, but I go by Bex. I hate Rebecca."

He nodded. "Bex. That's cool."

My heart raced. My name sounded absolutely perfect coming from his mouth.

"I'm Carter."

"Oh. That's my last name." It was a sign. It had to be a sign that we were meant to be.

"I know. I thought that was pretty cool."

"Yeah," I said, suddenly feeling awkward.

"Umm, can I come in?" he asked.

"Oh, of course," I said, stepping out of the doorway.

Carter came into the house and looked around. "Whoa, nice place."

"Thanks." I didn't know why I was saying thanks. It wasn't my house, but I didn't know what else to say.

Aunt Jeanie came out from the kitchen, wiping her hands on her apron. "Carter, nice to meet you." They shook hands, and she pointed him to the dining room table, where we would work.

"Bex, why don't you go on up and get your math book while I talk to Carter?"

"Sure," I said. That would give me a chance to check my appearance. In my bedroom, I stopped in front of my full-length mirror. I had on the same jeans and t-shirt I had worn to school, but now my t-shirt was wrinkled and my hair was totally frizzy.

I needed to fix myself up, but I had to be careful. If I made myself look too different, Carter would know that I had prettied myself up for him, and that wouldn't be cool. I put on a little lip gloss and ran a brush through my hair. Very subtle.

I dashed back downstairs to see Carter sitting at the table and Aunt Jeanie giving him the third degree. She looked up when I came down the stairs. "Bex, where's your book?"

"Oh," I said, feeling like a total idiot. Carter probably already thought I was stupid since I needed him to tutor me in the first place; now he probably thought I was a mental case.

I ran back up to grab my book and came back down. Carter sat at the head of the table, in Uncle Bob's chair. I took the seat to the left of him, trying not to make it obvious that I was moving the chair closer to him.

That was when I really got a good look at Carter. He looked like a bronze statue. He had tanned, sun-kissed skin and brown curly hair with blond highlights. His eyes were like bowls of chocolate pudding. I loved chocolate pudding. I inhaled his scent—Irish Spring soap.

He smiled at me, showing off his perfect teeth. "So, can you show me what chapter you guys are on?" Carter and I reached for my math book at the same time, and our hands touched. That was when I knew. He was the one, and I was in love for the first time. I'd never felt a shock of electricity when I touched someone before. Carter was the real deal. It was time for me to begin my very first love journal.

3

Love at First Sight

heart goes pitter pat

Dear Love Journal,

I met the love of my life today! I finally know what everyone's talking about when they say that being in love is the greatest feeling in the world. Carter is perfect for me. He gives me butterflies. The best part is that I think he likes me too. I think. He's sixteen and a sophomore in high school, but three years isn't that big a difference, especially when you're in love. Anyways, not only is Carter adorable, but he's really sweet and polite, kind of like Austin—oh, yeah, Austin . . .

I didn't know how I was supposed to concentrate with Carter sitting in front of me, but I did. Somehow he made me understand linear equations a little better. He was patient, and having one-on-one attention seemed to help. Unfortunately, our sessions were only an hour long, and that hour felt more like five minutes. I didn't want Carter to leave when our time was up.

Aunt Jeanie came back into the dining room when our session was over. "Thank you, Carter."

"No problem. Um, I'm not sure what kind of schedule you want to work on—two, three days a week?"

"I'm really, really behind, Carter," I said. Hey, it was the truth. "I think I need you to come every day."

Aunt Jeanie frowned. "Really, Bex?"

"Yes, Aunt Jeanie. At least for a little while. I need a lot of help. I got a *D,* remember."

She cringed at my utterance of the letter. "Are you available at this time Monday through Friday?"

"Sure," Carter answered.

My heart fluttered.

"Okay," Aunt Jeanie said. "We'll try that out for a few weeks until she gets a little better."

Carter pulled his backpack over one shoulder. "Sounds good. Okay, I'll see you tomorrow, Bex."

"Yeah. I'll walk you to the door."

Aunt Jeanie went back into the kitchen.

"Thanks for your help. I can already tell that it's helping me a lot." *Play it cool, Bex. Don't be too eager.*

"That's great. Then this is a win-win. You'll pass your math class, and I can save for a new car. We'll get you caught up in no time. Later."

I stood in the doorway and watched him climb into his old red convertible. The engine puttered a little before the car finally cranked up. I held my breath as I watched my future husband ride off into the sunset.

I squealed and ran up to my room to call my friends.

We were doing a video chat since I didn't have a cell phone. (I know, right. It should be illegal for me to not have a cell phone. I mean, what if I had an emergency or something?) Aunt Jeanie wouldn't even let me have a phone in my room. The only phones I could use in the house gave me no privacy, so I'd started video chatting with my friends. Of course they all had cell phones and gabbed with each other all day, leaving me out of many conversations.

Chirpy was already on. "Chirpy! I have big news!"

She squinted. "Are you wearing lip gloss?"

"Yes!"

"Well, I'll be a monkey's uncle. Why?"

"That's what I have to tell you, but I want to wait until the others are on."

Lily-Rose chimed in next and Marishca a few seconds later. "What's going on? Why are you wearing lip gloss?" she asked.

I sighed. "I'm wearing lip gloss because I am completely and utterly in love."

My exciting announcement was met by complete silence. I mean, I could hear crickets. "Hello? Did you guys hear what I said?"

"Not you," said Chirpy. "Not Miss All-You-Guys-Do-Is-Talk-About-Boys."

The others laughed at Chirpy's mockery of my newfound love.

"Guys, this isn't funny. I'm serious."

Marishca stopped laughing. "It's about time. Austin's a great guy."

"No. It's not Austin," I said.

The three of them looked like they'd seen a ghost pop up behind me or something.

Lily-Rose leaned forward. "Bex, who are you talking about then?"

"My new math tutor. His name is Carter."

Again silence. I tapped the computer screen. "Hello? Is this thing on?"

Chirpy cleared her throat. "Your math tutor. When did you meet this math tutor?"

"Today."

"You can't be in love wiz him already," Marishca said.

"What do you mean?" I asked. "Haven't you ever heard of love at first sight? You guys are supposed to be happy for me, *B.F.F.s.*"

Lily-Rose sighed. "It's not that, Bex. This is just weird. We've never seen you act this way before. You're usually so against love."

"I am not!" Really, they were acting like I was some kind of Debbie Downer. "I just don't like when you guys act like boys are the most important things in the world."

"Uh-huh," Chirpy said. "Welcome to the other side, Bex. You're officially one of us."

"Our little Bex is finally growing up," Marishca said excitedly.

"I don't know about this," Lily-Rose said skeptically, "but I have to get off now. I'll talk to you guys tomorrow."

We said our goodbyes and hung up. I practically floated to my closet. I had to pick out the perfect outfit for my next tutoring session.

4

Love Is In the Air

swoons

At school the next day, my friends demanded the 411. We
had banned the boys from the table so that we could have
girl talk. My friends were acting like me having a crush
was the biggest scandal of the century. I wasn't sure how I
felt about that.

I'd been on Cloud Nine all day. If this was what
love felt like—more, please! To top it off, the cafeteria was
serving tacos. The best part was that I had another tutoring
session with Carter to look forward to. That made the day
feel like Christmas was coming.

"So tell us everything about this boy," Chirpy said.

"Okay. His name is Carter, and I think the fact that
his first name is my last name is fate. He's sixteen, and he

goes to Lincoln High. He's saving money to buy a new car. How cool would it be to have a boyfriend with a car? He smells really good, and of course he's a wiz at math. That's all I know, I guess."

"Bex, he seems really nice," said Lily-Rose, "but he's in high school. I wouldn't get my hopes up if I were you."

"What does that have to do with anything?" I demanded. "I'm very mature for my age."

My friends all gave me the look. We all knew I was very *immature* for my age—at least in comparison to the other girls at school.

Chirpy squeezed sauce on her taco. "Bex, we just don't want you to get hurt, that's all. I mean, you just met this guy, and you're like head-over-heels in love. I'm just saying, don't flip your wig. For all you know, he could have a girlfriend."

Huh. That was something I hadn't thought about. "If he does, he's just going to have to dump her."

My friends sighed and exchanged glances. I hated when they did that. It meant they were all thinking the same thing about me. Right then they thought I was being stupid.

Marishca put her hand on her forehead. "Okay, Bex, but what about Austin? He's been your, what do you say, 'boy zat's a friend' for a while now. You can't just dump zee poor kid like zat."

"Austin had his chance, and he lost it. Besides, he's a boy. Carter is a real man."

My friends glanced at each other again.

I was tired of it. "Will you guys stop doing that?"

"Bex, we just don't want you to do anything stupid," Lily-Rose said.

"Trust me," I assured her. "I know exactly what I'm doing."

If I could go back in time, I would totally tell Future Bex to warn Past Bex that she had absolutely no idea what she was doing.

5

Bex + Carter = True Love

—feeling in love ♥

Dear Love Journal,

Today was my second session with Carter. I don't know how he does it, but he finds a way to make math easier to understand. I'm nowhere near where I need to be, but I'm definitely getting better. Anyway, I was determined to find out more about Carter. It would be a lot easier if Aunt Jeanie's house wasn't such a zoo.

After school I rushed home to get ready for my second tutoring session. I did all of my homework, except for math, took a shower, and then changed into one of the cutest outfits I have—a short-sleeved, hot-pink dress with a silver belt and ruffles at the bottom. Thanks to Aunt Jeanie, my closet was stocked with skirts and dresses which I usually hated, but at that moment I was glad I had them. Most times I opted for jeans or basketball shorts with a t-shirt, but I wanted to dress up for Carter. I had to show him that I wasn't just some kid. I was just as mature as those high-school girls.

I ran a brush through my hair. It wasn't as nice as I wanted it to be, but it would have to do. After putting on a little lip gloss, I contemplated other things, but I absolutely hated makeup. I was sure a guy like Carter liked girls with the natural look anyway.

I came down the stairs with my math book and notebook to wait for Carter. Aunt Jeanie was running around in a mad dash. She had to go to one of her society-lady meetings. She froze as I descended the stairs.

"Why are you dressed like that?" she asked, frowning.

I was surprised by her reaction because she was always pushing me to dress up and be more girly. She should have been pleased.

"What? I just want to look nice," I answered.

She raised her eyebrow at me. "Are you going somewhere?"

"No."

Her eyebrow went up higher. "Why would you dress up at home instead of dressing up for school? That makes no sense, Bex."

"Aunt Jeanie, I'm just practicing. Trying out some new looks. Is that a crime?"

She narrowed her eyes at me as if trying to uncover a secret I was keeping. "No. No, it's not." She went up the stairs, but I had a feeling that she knew I was up to something. I might have to start dressing up for school to throw her off. If she realized I was only dressing up for tutoring sessions, she'd figure it out. Worst case scenario— she would fire Carter.

I sat at the dining room table trying to look as lady-like as possible for Carter when he arrived. The kids, who were taking full advantage of Aunt Jeanie being preoccupied, were running all over the house like maniacs. It was kind of embarrassing. Hopefully Aunt Jeanie would make them go upstairs once Carter arrived.

The doorbell rang. I sat up nice and tall, remembering to use my best posture. Francois answered the door. Unfortunately, it wasn't Carter. It was Aunt Alice.

Now don't get me wrong, Aunt Alice is one of my favorite people in the world. She's my best grown-up friend, but I hadn't been expecting her.

"AUNT ALICE IS HERE!" Francois bellowed. The girls flew down the stairs squealing because everyone adored Aunt Alice. She was cool and sweet and smart. What wasn't there to love?

They almost knocked poor Aunt Alice over. I left the table and waited for the little monsters to back away so I could get my hug. Aunt Alice was beautiful—tall with long brown hair and brown eyes. She was my mom and Aunt Jeanie's baby sister. Aunt Alice was a photographer and traveled all over the world. I wanted to be a photojournalist when I grew up; that's why I wrote all the time. Aunt Alice had promised to take me on one of her trips this summer if I got good grades. So far, math was the only thing in the way of that.

Aunt Jeanie came pounding down the stairs. "Finally, you're here. I should have left twenty minutes ago."

Aunt Alice rolled her eyes. "Really? This is the thanks I get for babysitting for you on my vacation?"

"You're babysitting?" I asked.

"Yes." Aunt Jeanie answered for her younger sister. "I'm going to be spending a lot of time at the club over the next couple of weeks, getting ready for our annual benefit gala. Aunt Alice will come over in the evenings and watch you all until Uncle Bob gets home."

Normally, I would have been the designated babysitter, but Aunt Jeanie said that I had lost that "privilege" because of what had happened the last time I babysat. It's a long story. There was something about the police coming to the house . . . not a big deal really.

"Anyway, you all mind your Aunt Alice. I'll be back shortly," Aunt Jeanie said, rushing out of the door in a hurry.

"Aunt Alice, what are we going to do?" Reagan asked excitedly.

"This is a school night, so this is not going to be all fun and games. I want to check everyone's homework, and then we'll see about playing a game or something."

Aunt Alice was a lot of fun, but when she meant business, she meant business. The kids marched back upstairs to finish their homework.

I looked at Aunt Alice. "You want to spend your vacation babysitting those little termites?"

She laughed and pinched my cheek. "That's what family's for."

The doorbell rang again. It would definitely be Carter this time. "I'll get it. It's my tutor."

I opened the door as gracefully as I possibly could. "Carter!" I wanted to take that back immediately. I sounded way too eager. "Hi, Carter," I said, like a normal person.

"You looked nice," he said as he stepped inside.

My little heart did flip-flops in my chest. Once I had composed myself, I introduced him to Aunt Alice. "Carter, this is my Aunt Alice. Aunt Alice, this is Carter, my math tutor."

They shook hands. "Nice to meet you, Carter. I'm going to go up and help the kids with their homework. I'll let you guys get to work."

I led Carter to the dining room table. It was harder to concentrate then than it had been the first day. He had to explain the order of operations to me three times before I understood. He must have thought I was some kind of idiot.

He helped me with my homework and gave me a few word problems to do. I had a headache when our hour was up, but I felt like I was a little better at math.

I had to give it to Carter, he was all business. Not once during our session did he announce his undying love for me, even in my beautiful get-up. He was a true professional.

As I placed my papers in my notebook, Carter looked out of the sliding glass door that led to the patio. "Whoa, you guys have a basketball court?"

"Yeah."

"You ever play out there?"

"No. I never have anyone to play with. Sometimes Uncle Bob will play with me, but he doesn't have a lot of free time."

Carter gave me a sly look. "I'll play you."

"Right now?" I asked.

"Yeah. But I don't think you want to wear that," he said, eyeing my outfit.

"Right. Just give me a minute to change, and I'll be right back down."

I ran upstairs and threw on a t-shirt and some basketball shorts—what I should have been wearing in the first place. I pulled my hair back into a ponytail and grabbed my basketball from the closet. I don't think I had fully processed the fact that I was about to play basketball with the love of my life.

I told Aunt Alice that we would be out back, and I led Carter to the court. He couldn't stay too long, so we were playing to thirty points. Carter was great at basketball, but it wasn't a fair game. How was I supposed to concentrate when he looked so cute? He had kicked my butt, earning 31 points to my 18.

He tossed me the ball as he slid his backpack over his shoulders. "You're pretty good, Bex. You like sports?"

"Yeah. I play everything. I need to bring my math grade up so I can stay on the soccer team."

"Well, we're going to make that happen. Don't worry." Then you'll never guess what he did—he winked at me!

"You owe me a rematch," I said as he exited the yard. Very smooth, Bex.

"You got it," he called over his shoulder. "See you tomorrow."

Yes, tomorrow. I couldn't wait.

6

Carnival Madness

—feeling nervous ☹

Dear Love Journal,

This carnival has given me a great idea. It's a scary idea, but a great one. I hope he says yes.

The following morning Principal Radcliff called all of the eighth graders into the auditorium. We were to break into groups to begin planning our booths for the carnival. Chirpy, Lily-Rose, Marishca, Maverick, Jeeves, and I found a nice spot on the floor where we could work. Maverick pulled out a sheet of paper and began sketching. We needed to decide how we would decorate.

"I think it would be really cool to paint stars and moons all over it," Lily-Rose was saying, when we were rudely interrupted. Ava G. had walked right through the circle we were sitting in. She'd even poked a hole in our paper with her high-heeled shoe. The other Avas, Ava T. and Ava M., stood behind her.

"What's wrong with you?" I shouted. "Don't you see us working here?"

"No," she answered. "Losers are invisible to me, loser."

The other Avas giggled as if she had said the funniest thing in the world. She was totally *not* funny.

"What kind of booth are you geeks doing?" Ava G. asked.

"None of your business," Marishca said. "Keep it moving."

"What are you guys doing?" Jeeves asked her. I scowled at him. We needed to ignore her so they would leave.

"We are doing a beauty booth where people can stop and get makeovers. I hope you guys take advantage of it, especially you, Bex," she said nastily.

"Get out of here, Ava! We're trying to work!"

"Calm down, dork. We'll leave you alone to work on your silly booth. I bet ours earns more money than yours."

She flicked her long jet-black hair over her shoulder and walked away with her followers on her heels.

Santiago sighed. "Why do the beautiful ones have to be so mean?"

No matter how awful Ava was, all the boys liked her, which I found quite lame. Ava could get away with murder. She was a pretty girl—sparkling green eyes set off by dark hair—but as pretty as she was, she was even uglier on the inside. Even though she was awful, everyone gave her everything she wanted. Such is life, as my nana would say.

Chirpy crumpled the torn sheet of paper. "She's right, you guys. This is a stupid idea."

"No, it's not. Just because Ava says something doesn't make it so. I think it's a great idea." I really didn't, but I was determined to do it now that Ava had challenged us. Makeover booth . . . I wished someone would figure out a way to give personality makeovers.

We spent the rest of the planning time sketching another booth, and we had come up with some great ideas of how to decorate it. That was the easy part. At lunch time a more complicated subject came up.

"You know that it's Lincoln Middle tradition to bring a date to the carnival, right?" Lily-Rose asked.

That was fine for everyone at the table—except for me and Santiago, they were all going out with people.

"You should ask Austin, Bex," Marishca suggested.

"No. I'm going to ask Carter."

Chirpy almost choked on her chocolate milk. "What? Bex, I don't think that's a good idea."

"Why not?" Jeeves asked. "And who's Carter?"

"Carter is Bex's math tutor, whom she thinks she's in love with," Lily-Rose said. The way she said it made it sound so stupid.

"And he's sixteen," Marishca added.

I rolled my eyes. "Thanks girls, for sharing all my business."

"Bex, he's too old for you," Jeeves said.

"There's less than three years between us. What does age matter anyway?"

Maverick shook his head. "Don't ask him. He'll break your heart."

"I have to agree," said Santiago. "High-school boys don't want to date girls in middle school. I mean that's one

45

of the best parts of high school—high-school girls." Then he yelped and grabbed his shin because someone had kicked him underneath the table. "Who did that?"

See why boys didn't need to be involved in girl talk? Boys knew nothing about boys!

My third session with Carter was going splendidly until the doorbell rang. Aunt Jeanie was flying around the house getting things ready before she left to go to her country club. Aunt Alice opened the door. Much to my dismay, Mrs. Groves and Ava entered carrying some kind of metal machines.

"Jeanie's in the kitchen," Aunt Alice told them.

Mrs. Groves and Ava stopped in the dining room on their way to the kitchen. "Well, what do we have here?" Mrs. Groves asked. She was one of the nosiest people I knew.

"This is Carter, my math tutor," I answered. "Carter, this is my aunt's friend Mrs. Groves, and that's—" I stared at Ava as if I were trying to remember her name. She scowled at me. "Oh yeah, Ava, I think it is."

Ava and I had a weird relationship. Her mother and Aunt Jeanie were best friends. They forced us to hang out together outside of school. Deep down inside, Aunt Jeanie would have liked me to be like Ava, but that would never, ever, ever, ever, not in a million years, ever happen.

"Nice to meet you," Carter said politely. I could tell he was such a gentleman.

"Well, don't let us disturb you. We just came to drop these off for your aunt," Mrs. Groves said before they went into the kitchen. Thankfully they left a moment later, but not before Ava shot me an ice-cold look.

I had been working up the nerve during our tutoring session to ask Carter to be my date for the carnival. It was almost time for him to leave, so I had to act fast.

"Carter, can I ask you something?"

"Sure," he said, looking at me expectantly. His eyes seemed even browner then, and there were little flecks of copper . . .

"Bex?"

"Oh yeah, I wanted to know—" *Ask him, Bex. Just blurt it out!* "When I'm doing a linear equation, do I multiply or divide first?"

Stupid, stupid, stupid! I knew the answer to that question. Carter *knew* I knew the answer to that question, but because he was such a sweetie he just smiled and said, "Please Excuse My Dear Aunt Sally. You multiply first."

Duh.

"Thanks. I'll remember that." So I chickened out. That was just a warm-up. I would ask him the next day.

That night I had the most wonderful dream I had ever had. Carter and I were married, and we lived in Australia with our three kids: Venus, Serena, and Beckham. We were famous athletes, and Bexter was our celebrity couple name (cute, huh?). I was a professional soccer player, and Carter was a professional basketball player. We lived in a cool-looking house made out of logs out in the middle of nowhere, away from our herds of adoring fans.

Sigh. A girl can dream can't she?

Friday night was my turn to host the sleepover. I was kind of excited because I had told my friends to come right when my tutoring session would be over so that I could introduce them to Carter. Maybe once they saw him, they'd understand why I was so in love.

We'd had another good session. Carter gave me a practice test since I'd be having a real test the following week in Mr. Hawthorne's class. Carter scored the test, and I'd earned a 76%. It wasn't great, but it was passing and definitely better than what I'd been getting. Still, I had work to do.

The doorbell rang, and I hopped up. "Carter, my friends are here. I want you to meet them."

"Okay," Carter said, tossing his things into his backpack.

I opened the front door. Chirpy, Marishca, and Lily-Rose stood there with their duffle bags, grinning from ear to ear.

"Hey, guys," I said.

Chirpy stepped inside and dropped her duffle bag on the ground. "Well, well, well, what do we have here?" She circled Carter, eyeing him suspiciously.

He cleared his throat and extended his hand to her. "Um, hi, I'm Carter."

Chirpy slapped his hand away. "Don't play that nice-boy routine with me. I know what high-school boys are like. My cousin's a high-school boy and he's a cretin."

"Chirpy!" I couldn't believe her. She was totally embarrassing me. "Ignore her, Carter. That's Marishca and this is Lily-Rose." At least they acted normal and shook his hand.

"Nice to meet you guys. I'll see you Monday, Bex."

Ah, Monday. That meant I would have to go two whole days without seeing him. I didn't think I could survive that.

The girls and I followed him onto the porch where he fished his car keys out of his pocket. I followed him down the walkway.

"Carter, can I ask you something?"

He stopped and leaned against his car. "Sure. What's up?"

I felt as if someone was watching me. I turned to see my three friends only a few feet away. "Do you guys mind?" It had taken me all day to muster up the courage to ask Carter this question. They were making me nervous.

They each took a step back. "Don't worry. We can't hear you," Lily-Rose said.

I sighed and lowered my voice. It was now or never. "Carter, I wanted to know if you would like to go to my school's carnival with me. Kind of like my date, but not really because I'm not allowed to date yet, but I guess it's not really a date, just a boy and a girl hanging out and . . ." I stopped talking because I realized I was rambling.

Carter paused for a second, and looked at the ground. I got ready for a major rejection. What was I thinking asking a boy out? What was wrong with me?

"Bex, I'd love to," Carter answered.

I felt like running across the lawn and doing cartwheels, but I didn't because Carter would think I was a lunatic. "Great. So, I guess I'll see you later."

Carter flashed me that gorgeous smile and then took off. What had I been afraid of? He was my soulmate. Of course he wasn't going to say no.

When I turned around, my friends were nowhere to be seen. I found them in my room, lounging on my bed.

"Bex, are you okay?" Marishca asked.

I threw myself on the bed in the middle of them, feeling like I was floating on air. "Sure, I'm okay."

The girls exchanged glances and shook their heads.

"Just think. When we get married, he'll be Mr. Carter Carter," I said dreamily.

"Uh, Bex? Why would he take your last name?" Chirpy asked.

"Chirpy, really, that's the least of our worries. Look at her. We've totally lost her," Lily-Rose replied.

"What are you guys talking about? You all have boyfriends. Why is it a problem because I have one?" I demanded.

Marishca looked down at me. "First of all, you do not have a boyfriend, and second of all, none of us acted the way you're acting—like a lovesick puppy. Zis isn't a good look. I'm worried about you, Bex."

I sat up. "You guys are totally exaggerating. I get it. You're not used to me being a part of a couple. This is new to you, but it's not like I'm acting crazy or something. Does anybody know how much it costs to get a tattoo?"

"What?" They all shouted at the same time.

"Think about it. I could get his name tattooed right here on my arm," I explained. "If we ever break up, which we won't, Carter is still my last name, so I won't look stupid."

"Yeah, and then your aunt will send you to military school," Chirpy reminded me.

"That's true. I'll get it when I'm older."

"Bex, getting someone's name tattooed on you is the stupidest idea ever. This Carter guy is making you looney," Lily-Rose said.

"You guys are just jealous because Carter's a high-school guy and you're going out children."

Chirpy rolled her eyes. "Bex, you're not dating anybody. Now, no more boy talk. Let's talk about something else."

Marishca turned some music on, and the girls talked about some TV show they were watching, but I didn't participate. I was too busy imagining what it would be like spending a night at the carnival with Carter.

7

Stalkerish

hangs head in shame

Dear Love Journal,

I spent my entire Saturday thinking about Carter. I think I was having Carter withdrawals. The entire day I thought about where he was, what he was doing, and who he was with. When I couldn't take it anymore, I did some investigating around the neighborhood. Molly Hayes, who lives down the street, goes to Lincoln High. I asked her if she knew Carter, and she said she knew him very well. She told me he liked to hang out at the wave pool at Do Something. Do Something was a place where kids hang out. They have go-carts, rock climbing, arcade games, laser-tag, and a wave pool. Carter usually went there on Sundays

with his friends. So since it had been an entire day since I'd seen him. I went there. That's not weird at all. Right?

On Sunday afternoon I put on my one-piece bathing suit, which I covered with a black t-shirt and denim shorts. There was no way Carter, or any boy for that matter, was about to see me in my bathing suit.

I didn't want to go alone, and I definitely couldn't ask Chirpy, Marishca, or Lily-Rose to go with me because they were so not being supportive, so I asked my other friend, Geraldine, to come along. I had met Geraldine last Spring. I have to admit that she was a little out there, but I really, really liked her.

Geraldine's mother dropped her off. She stood on the porch wearing a vest made out of candy-printed fabric. Geraldine made her own vests that she wore all the time. Her long brown hair was pulled back into a ponytail. She grinned, exposing her purple braces. "Thanks for inviting me, Bex. This is going to be a blast!"

My Uncle Bob dropped us off at Do Something and we went out to the wave pool. We had to purchase a plastic bracelet to get into the gate where the wave pool was located.

After Geraldine and I bought our bracelets, I put on some shades and looked around for Carter. I didn't see him anywhere. Geraldine and I edged the tall metal fence, keeping our eyes open.

I saw tons of kids with boogie boards riding the waves manufactured by the pool. It looked like a lot of fun, but I was focused on one thing.

I dragged Geraldine behind a tall potted plant while I scoured the wave pool for Carter. At last I spotted him wearing a black wetsuit that cut off at the knees. With his chocolate-colored hair slicked back, he maneuvered the waves flawlessly.

I grabbed Geraldine's arm. "That's him. The one in the black wetsuit." I was probably acting like I had seen a celebrity, but that's what it felt like.

Geraldine looked in Carter's direction. "Oh. Okay. Let's go talk to him." She stood and walked away.

I pulled her back. "Are you crazy? We can't talk to him. I don't want him to know I'm here."

Geraldine frowned. "Then why did you tell me to wear a bathing suit? Why are you wearing a bathing suit?"

"Just in case he saw us, I could pretend we were here to swim. Being caught at a pool in regular clothes, it would have looked like I was just here to see him."

"Then why are we here?"

"To watch him."

Geraldine stared at me for a moment. "Bex, you're a stalker."

"What? I am not!" I just wanted to see Carter. She was making it sound creepy.

"Yes, you are, and I think we should leave," Geraldine said, heading for the exit.

I sighed and followed behind her. Geraldine was the strangest person I knew. I didn't care what she thought.

When we were almost to the exit, someone called my name.

"Bex?"

I turned to see Carter drying himself off with a towel. "Oh, hey, Carter. What a surprise!" I tried to take deep breaths because my heart was racing.

"Yeah. What are you doing here?" he asked.

"I came to swim in the wave pool, of course."

He frowned. "Then why are you leaving?"

"Um . . . I'm tired."

"But you're not even wet," he said.

"Uhh," I said, struggling for an answer. Thankfully Geraldine saved me.

"Hello, I'm Geraldine Cordelia Ulysses, Bex's best friend," Geraldine said as she offered Carter her hand.

Carter shook it. "Nice to meet you."

"Listen, the guys and I are going to the snack bar for some fries."

"Oh, I love fries," I answered casually.

"Yeah? Come on over."

I don't remember if I replied to him verbally, or nodded or what. I just know that my heart was doing the happy dance in my chest, and the next thing I knew Geraldine and I were sitting with Carter and his friends at a table in the snack bar area.

I never had a problem getting along with boys, but I wasn't sure how to act around high-school guys.

"Here you go," Carter said, placing a carton of fries in front of me. "This is a treat for all the progress you've made in just one week."

"Thanks, Carter." I had been sure to tell him no ketchup because Geraldine has a ketchup phobia. (I know, right?)

He handed Geraldine a bottle of water because that was all she wanted. Geraldine is a very picky eater.

"So where do you go to school?" asked a blond guy.

"Lincoln Middle," I answered.

"I go to school at home," Geraldine replied because she was home-schooled. So far she had been cool. I prayed she didn't say or do anything weird.

"That's cool," the boy said. "You got the best tutor in town. Carter helps me with my math a lot. He's a wiz."

"He's the best," I said. You won't believe what Carter did then—he winked at me again. I thought I would melt right there on the spot.

"I'm really nervous about my next test, though."

"Don't be worried," Carter assured me. "You got this. Just remember, if you do something on one side of an equation, you have to do the same thing to the other side."

That's what I liked the most about Carter. He was patient and caring. Even though he wasn't on the clock, he was still giving tips. When he told me not to worry, all my anxiety went away.

I didn't have long before Uncle Bob would be picking us up. Aunt Jeanie had said I had to be home in time for dinner.

"I'm excited about our session tomorrow," I told Carter. "I love math now." Did I sound like a total dork? No, I didn't. I sounded exceptionally cool.

"Yeah, it's cool. You're a good tutee," he said, as if I needed any more proof that he liked me as much as I liked him.

I hated that we had to leave, but I gave Carter a quick goodbye, then Geraldine and I went to the front of the building to wait for Uncle Bob.

"So what do you think?" I asked Geraldine as we waited. "Cute, huh?"

"He's okay. Not really my type."

I didn't even want to guess what her type was. I didn't understand how any girl could think Carter was just "okay." He was the perfect boy prototype.

"Bex, I hate to say it, but I'm with Geraldine on this one," Lily-Rose said on Monday morning. "That was a bit stalkerish."

We were standing in front of her locker, and I had made the mistake of telling her what had happened at the wave pool, thinking she would be happy for me.

"How can you say that?"

Lily-Rose sighed. "You asked around for information about him. You went to a place where he hangs out. You hid from him and watched him from behind a shrub when he didn't know you were there. Put yourself in

60

his shoes. What if someone were watching you without you knowing? Wouldn't you find that a little creepy?"

Okay, I'll admit that when she laid it out like that, it did sound a little kooky, but it had given me another chance to see Carter. I made up my mind right then and there that I'd stop talking to my friends about him. They just didn't get it. Why should I expect middle-school kids to understand a high-school relationship anyway?

"You just don't understand, Lily-Rose. Maybe one day you will."

She put her hand on my shoulder. "Bex, I'm really worried about you. This whole Carter thing isn't healthy."

She sounded like a therapist. I wasn't crazy. I was just a girl in love. Why did they have a problem with that?

"Don't worry about me, Lily-Rose. I know what I'm doing," I reassured her.

The bell rang, and we had to get to class. Lily-Rose gave me a sympathetic look before walking away. What was her problem?

At lunch we talked more about the fortune-telling booth. I hoped this silly booth didn't take too much time away from me hanging out with Carter at the carnival. I'd already had a dream of us going through the haunted house together. I'd grab onto his arm and pretend to be afraid when I really wasn't. Cheesy haunted houses never scared me, but it would be the perfect opportunity to get close to Carter.

It was decided that Marishca would tell fortunes from a crystal ball because of her accent. "I'm sure I can find a crystal ball at one of zose antique shops."

Chirpy would be the palm reader. Lily-Rose would read cards. Santiago was going to be the money collector. Jeeves would stand in front of the booth in his tux and call people over, and Maverick would walk through the crowd inviting people to our booth.

"Earth to Bex," Jeeves said, waving his hand in my face.

"What?"

"What are you going to do for the booth?" he asked. "You're the only one who doesn't have a job yet."

"Umm . . . you guys pretty much have it covered. I'll do my part before the carnival. I'll be in charge of decorating the booth."

"Cool," Lily-Rose said. "I think our booth is really going to rock!"

Truth be told, I was caring less and less about the booth and more and more about having fun with Carter, but I would never, ever tell my friends that.

8

I Declare War

growls

Dear Love Journal,

You won't believe what happened in my tutoring session. Why can't anything ever go right for me? Auuugggghhhhhh! I can't even write about it!

Monday's tutoring session was going along just fine until the doorbell rang. Aunt Alice answered it. Mrs. Groves and Ava stepped in. I figured they were there to drop something off for the charity event, but I was wrong, so wrong. Ava had her leather backpack slung over one shoulder. I was confused. I was even more confused when she sat at the dining room table on the other side of Carter.

"Sorry I'm late. It's my mother's fault," she said, grinning at Carter.

"What are you doing?" I demanded.

Just then Aunt Jeanie came from the kitchen carrying her purse. "Oh, yes. I forgot to tell you. Ava needs a little help in math too. She'll be joining in on your sessions. Carter doesn't mind."

I couldn't believe what I was hearing. Ava got straight A's in math and everything else. She was one of those people who were just good at everything except for being nice. I called shenanigans.

I glared at Ava, and she narrowed her eyes at me. We both knew she needed math tutoring like she needed another layer of gloss on her lips.

"Yes," Mrs. Groves said. "I don't know what happened. Ava's always done great in math, and all of a sudden last week she started having a hard time. We want to get her help now before she falls behind. My Ava has never gotten anything less than an A."

I couldn't believe her. She didn't take her gaze off me even as she opened her math book to the chapter we were on.

"Carter, like always, help yourself to anything in the fridge," Aunt Jeanie said.

"Ava, I'll be back to pick you up after we're done at the club," Mrs. Groves announced as she and Aunt Jeanie left, chatting away.

"I'll be in the kitchen getting dinner started," Aunt Alice told us. "Let me know if you need anything."

"Okay, Aunt Alice," I replied, still staring at Ava.

"All right," Carter said. "Let's start on page 118, problem number one."

Ava and I both found the page, and Carter began to explain. He sat at the head of the table with Ava and me on either side of him. As he spoke, I noticed Ava inching her chair closer and closer to him. I needed to concentrate, and she was totally distracting me. Ava had an advantage: she really didn't need to pay attention to Carter's explanations, but I did. I needed to bring up my grade.

I couldn't let her get closer to Carter than me, though. Every time she moved her chair over an inch, I moved mine over two inches. Pretty soon we'd both be sitting on his lap.

"What are you guys doing?" Carter asked once we were so close we couldn't get any closer.

"Uh, I wanted to move closer so I can hear you better," I said.

"I moved closer because I like the way you smell," Ava said boldly.

My jaw almost hit the table. I couldn't believe she was being so flirtatious and straightforward with him. Who does that?

Carter cleared his throat. "I'm going to go into the kitchen and get a drink of water."

"I'll get it for you," I offered.

"No, that's all right. I'll get it," he insisted.

"I can't believe you," I told Ava once Carter was out of the room. "You're failing math on purpose just to get tutored by a cute boy. Do you have any idea how pathetic that is?"

"What's pathetic is you thinking a boy like Carter would be interested in you. I see the way you drool over him."

I was about to say something back, but Carter returned.

"Okay, where were we?" he asked after taking a swig from the water bottle.

The rest of the lesson was a blur. It was hard enough for me to focus with Carter teaching me, but now with Ava sitting across from me shooting me dirty looks it was nearly impossible. How was I supposed to bring my math grade up now?

Tuesday's tutoring session was even worse. Mrs. Groves and Aunt Jeanie stayed at the country club long after our tutoring session ended, which meant that Ava had stayed for dinner. I hoped that didn't become a habit, because it was inhumane punishment.

Aunt Alice had just come from upstairs, solving some crisis the Brat Squad was having, when she stopped by the dining room table to check on us.

"How about hot dogs for dinner?" she asked.

"Aunt Alice, Aunt Jeanie left a squash-and-cauliflower casserole in the freezer." I wanted to gag just saying it. "She doesn't let us eat hot dogs."

As much as I would have loved to have a good hot dog for dinner, I knew Aunt Jeanie would hit the roof if she found out. I didn't want her and Aunt Alice to fight. She might not let Aunt Alice babysit anymore.

"Well, Aunt Jeanie doesn't have to know about it, does she? Do you guys like hot dogs?" she asked Carter and Ava.

"I wouldn't eat one for a million bucks. Do you have any idea what's in those things?" Ava asked, crinkling her perfect little button nose.

"Nope," Carter answered, "and I don't want to know. I love hot dogs."

"Oh, *hot dogs*!" Ava said. "I thought you said snot hogs. I absolutely love hot dogs."

So pathetic.

"Really, Ava?" I asked. "You thought she said snot hogs? Why would she say that?"

Ava shot me eye daggers, but I stood my ground.

"Great. I'm going to run to the store and grab some. Bex, keep an eye on the kids until I get back. I won't be long. Twenty minutes tops." Aunt Alice said.

We both knew good and well that I wasn't allowed to be in charge of the kids anymore, but Aunt Alice was out of the door before I could protest.

Carter assigned Ava and me some practice problems to complete. I had two done when I heard a blood-curdling scream come from upstairs. I continued to work, pretending not to hear it.

"Uh, Bex, shouldn't you go check on that?" Ava asked.

"No." I knew it was Francois. He yelled like that all the time for the stupidest reasons.

He screamed again.

"Maybe you should check on that," Carter said.

I didn't want to leave him alone with Ava, not even for a second, but I also didn't want him to think that I was an insensitive jerk who didn't care about her family. Besides, there was a slight chance that something was really wrong.

I dashed up the stairs as quickly as possible so I could return to my tutoring session promptly. Another scream came from Priscilla and Penelope's bedroom.

"What are you guys doing?" I asked from the doorway.

Priscilla, Penelope, and Reagan had poor Francois tied to an ironing board with jump ropes.

"Untie him right now!" I demanded.

"We can't!" Ray said. "He invaded our privacy."

"What?" I didn't have time for this. I needed to get back downstairs.

"Yeah," Penelope said. "We were telling secrets, and he was hiding under the bed, listening. He's a dirty sneak."

"Listen, I so cannot deal with this right now. Let him go, and Francois, leave them alone. Stop invading their privacy," I said, although I had no idea what ten- and seven-year-olds needed to be private about.

"We're never going to let him go," Ray said.

That was when I lost it. *"I SAID LET HIM GO!"*

The girls' eyes widened, and they hurriedly untied the ropes. I felt awful for yelling at them, but it had worked.

Once Francois was free, he sat there rubbing his arms, and all four kids stared at me.

"Look, guys, I'm sorry I yelled. I'm just under a lot of pressure right now. You'll understand when you're older. I'll make it up to you. Love you. Bye."

I dashed back downstairs, and I made it back just in time. Ava was leaning in so close to Carter, she could kiss him if she wanted to.

I cleared my throat as I entered the dining room.

"Is everything okay?" Carter asked.

"Yeah, everything's okay *upstairs*," I answered.

Aunt Alice came back and began to make hot dogs. I was happy that Carter had stayed for dinner, although eating with the Brat Squad wasn't romantic at all. Carter was cool about it though. We listened to Aunt Alice tell us stories about her travels. I never got tired of listening to her experiences. I wanted a job like that so badly.

I watched as Ava the Liar removed the hot dog from the bun and ate only the bread. Strange move for a hot dog lover.

Carter left right after dinner, and unfortunately Ava stayed because her mother wasn't back yet.

"If you think you're going to get him to like you, you'd better think again," she whispered to me as we cleared the table. "Give me a few days, and he'll be all mine."

Little did she know that Carter and I were going to the carnival together, and I couldn't wait for her to find out.

9

Ava + (Bex + Carter) = Not Cool

—feeling frustrated ☹

Dear Love Journal,

Of all the guys in the world. Why does Ava have to pick the one that I like? Although I know Carter likes me, I'm a little worried. Ava's so pretty. All the boys like her. Besides that, she always gets what she wants.

Ava and I sat across from each other at the dining room table, staring each other down. Carter wasn't due for another fifteen minutes, but we both wanted to be ready and waiting for him.

"What about Brayden?" I asked. Brayden was a boy at our school Ava was supposed to be going out with.

"Brayden is cute and everything, but he's disposable. What about Austin?"

"What about him?"

Ava flicked her hair over her shoulder. "You know, his mother is friends with your aunt and my mother. I could easily get his number and tell him how you're fawning all over your math tutor."

"Do it. Austin's not my boyfriend anyway. We're just friends," I said.

"We'll see," Ava said.

Carter arrived, and he began to review what we had learned in math class that day. I needed that because I was completely lost. Ava, on the other hand, didn't need this because she was great in math, so she decided to completely ruin our tutoring session.

"Carter, I'm sorry to interrupt," she said sweetly, "but did you know that Bex gets in trouble all the time? I mean, she's always in detention."

That was completely untrue. It had been two weeks since I'd had a detention.

"Did you know that Ava is the meanest girl in school?" I asked. "She's downright *evil*."

"Did Bex tell you that during lunch she sits at a table that she named the Awesome Possum table? Isn't that the lamest thing you ever heard?"

Carter smiled. "Actually, I think it's pretty cute."

I smirked at Ava. "Did Ava tell you that in the fifth grade she puked in the middle of the awards assembly? Right on stage. They had to shut the cafeteria down."

Ava huffed. "Did Bex tell you that in the first grade she used to pick her nose and eat whatever she found? I think she still does it."

"I do not!" I said, pounding the table.

Carter pushed his chair away from the table. "You know what? I'm going to grab a snack and let you two cool down. I'll be back."

"What is wrong with you?" I asked Ava once Carter had disappeared into the kitchen.

"I'm just letting him know what kind of loser you are," Ava answered.

"Well knock it off. He's going to think we're both crazy."

Ava folded her arms across her chest. "Bex Carter, this is one war you're not going to win. I always win. You are never going to beat me, so just give it up."

"Oh yeah? Did you know that Carter's going to the carnival with me?" I asked.

Ava scoffed. "Yeah right. You're such a liar."

"Am I? Ask him yourself."

Ava unzipped her purse and took out a tube of lip gloss. "You know what, Bex? It doesn't matter. By the time the carnival comes around, he'll be going with me, and he won't even remember who you are."

I turned the page in my math book to begin a practice problem. It didn't make any sense to argue with Ava. She'd get the picture when I was strolling through the carnival hand in hand with Carter. What was taking him so long in the kitchen anyway?

He came back a few minutes later shoving the last piece of a brownie in his mouth. "Your Aunt Alice makes killer brownies."

Yes, she does, and Aunt Jeanie was going to flip out about the brownies just like she'd flipped about the hot dogs. The Triple Terrors were the biggest tattlers I knew. They could never keep a secret.

Carter wrapped up our lesson and high-tailed it out of there like he couldn't get out of the house fast enough. Thanks a lot, Ava!

10

Making Progress

—feeling proud ☺

Friday morning I waited with anticipation as Mr. Hawthorne passed back the math tests we had taken the day before. It was the first test I'd taken since I'd begun my tutoring sessions with Carter. I really had to make progress. I didn't want to let him or Aunt Jeanie down, I had to bring up my grade, and I had to stay on the soccer team.

     I closed my eyes and held my hands out to receive my test. "Good improvement, Bex," I heard Mr. Hawthorne say as he placed my math test in my hands. I took a deep breath and opened my eyes. In thick red letters at the top of my page was written "82%". I was ecstatic. I'd made it out of the seventies. Maybe on the next test I could score at least a ninety. For a girl who had been previously scoring in the forties and fifties, I was very proud of myself, and I hoped Carter would be too.

At lunch there was more carnival talk. I hadn't given much thought to the booth or how I would decorate it. I had actually forgotten that I'd volunteered to do that.

"So," Santiago said, "they're opening the carnival grounds this weekend from eleven until two for everyone to decorate their booths. I have to work on my website design business that day."

"I have a swim meet," Chirpy said.

"Violin lessons," Lily-Rose chimed in.

"Gymnastics competizhun," said Marishca.

"I have drum lessons," Maverick said.

"I have baseball," said Jeeves.

"Guys, don't worry. I got this," I reassured them.

"Are you sure, Bex?" Jeeves asked.

"Sure I'm sure." I mean how hard could it be? I'd make some moons and stars. Decorate a poster. Paint a sign or something. It'd only be a few hours, and then I'd be free to spend the carnival with Carter while my friends ran the booth. I didn't mind getting my part out of the way ahead of time. "Don't worry. I'll make sure it looks amazing."

Saturday morning I woke up at around ten o'clock. I was surprised that Aunt Jeanie hadn't woken me. She never let anyone sleep past eight o'clock, even on the weekends. She said winners were early risers.

I dragged myself out of bed and ran downstairs for some breakfast. I discovered why Aunt Jeanie hadn't woken me up. She had already left the house, and Aunt Alice sat at the table with the Brat Squad finishing up breakfast.

"There's Sleeping Ugly," Francois said, sticking his tongue out at me. Children.

"Bex, we saved you some pancakes," Aunt Alice said, giving me a kiss as she cleared the table.

I took a seat as she placed three heart-shaped pancakes on my plate. "Thanks."

"No problem. Kids, help me clear the table," Aunt Alice ordered.

Obediently, the kids stacked silverware on the dirty dishes and proceeded to carry them to the kitchen. The doorbell rang.

"I'll get it," Priscilla called, running to the door.

"See who it is before you open it," I told her.

"Oh, it's your math teacher," Priscilla called.

Huh? Mr. Hawthorne?

But it wasn't Mr. Hawthorne. Imagine my surprise when Carter entered the dining room.

I put my fork down and hoped there was no food on my face. "Carter, what are you doing here? We don't have sessions on Saturdays." It's not that I wasn't happy to see him, but I was wearing my pink elephant pajamas and I still had bed-hair. I wanted to crawl underneath the table.

"I know. I just thought it would be cool if I could hang out a bit," he answered.

Cool? Was he kidding me? That would be fantastic! If my friends were there, they'd be eating their words. Carter couldn't stand to be away from me. That was definitely a sign of true love.

Aunt Alice came from the kitchen to grab more stuff from the table. "Oh, Carter. I thought you only came during the week."

"Yeah, I just wanted to hang out. Maybe Bex and I could shoot some hoops or something. If she wants we can practice a little math since she's doing so much better."

"Sure, make yourself at home," Aunt Alice said.

Unfortunately my sister and cousins thought that Carter was there to see them.

"Will you play Marco Polo with us?" Ray asked.

"I didn't bring my swim trunks," Carter answered.

"We don't have to play it in the pool," Ray suggested.

"No, let us do your hair," Penelope said. She and Priscilla loved to play beauty salon.

"Ummm . . ." Carter said.

Aunt Alice saved the day. "Uh-uh. Go get ready for ballet, girls. And Francois, I'm dropping you off for your cello lessons."

"Awww," the kids moaned as they moped upstairs.

"I'll be back," Aunt Alice told us. "Your Uncle Bob is working in his office if you need anything, but don't disturb him unless it's an absolute emergency. I think he's on a long conference call."

Uncle Bob's office was actually his man cave, and I was pretty sure he wasn't working.

I cleared my spot at the table, and Aunt Alice left with the kids to get them to their lessons. That meant Carter and I were practically alone in the house and would be for approximately thirty minutes. I suddenly felt nervous.

"Ummm . . . do you like to play pool?" I asked.

"Sure. You guys have a table?"

"Yep. Let me change and then we'll play." I ran up to my room and contemplated for a moment over what I should wear. I settled on a pair of jeans and a T-shirt with a huge B on the front.

Once I was dressed I led Carter to the entertainment room where the pool table was held. We spent the afternoon playing pool and basketball, and we even got a head start on the next chapter in math. Normally I would abhor doing school work on a Saturday; I liked to leave my weekend homework until the last minute on Sunday evenings, but doing math with Carter didn't feel like doing work at all.

He reminded me a lot of Austin. He didn't make me nervous and we could just relax and have normal fun with no pressure. Carter was however, a more mature and sophisticated version of Austin. He had a job, a car, and was super smart.

I was having a great day spending time with Carter, but I couldn't shake this nagging feeling that I was forgetting something.

Carter and I sat on the patio sipping lemonade after the math session.

"It must be nice to live like this all the time. The rich kids at school, they don't have to work for cars. Their parents just give them one when they turn sixteen. I'm talking luxury sports cars. You're lucky, Bex," Carter said as he stared out at the pool.

I shrugged. "It's not really mine. My sister and I are just here for the time being."

"Why's that?" Carter asked.

Usually, I didn't like talking about my parents, but if Carter and I were going to be a couple, he should know these things. "My dad's in jail for stealing money from his job," I said quickly. "When he gets out, we'll go live with him."

"Oh," was all Carter said. I prayed he wouldn't ask about my mother. Thankfully he didn't.

Later that afternoon, Aunt Alice announced that she was baking a chocolate cake. I guess she was in the mood to have a huge blowout fight with Aunt Jeanie this weekend, because that's what was going to happen. Carter said he wanted to learn how to bake a cake, which I thought was pretty cool, so he helped Aunt Alice. I wasn't too interested in learning how to make a cake, but I watched. Carter looked super cute wearing an apron with flour on his face.

While the cake was in the oven, Carter and I sat on either side of Aunt Alice on the sofa while she showed us slides from her latest photo shoots. Her pictures were amazing. I hoped I could be half as good as she was when I became a photojournalist.

Aunt Jeanie came home later that evening looking a little, well . . . perturbed.

"What's wrong, Jeanie?" Aunt Alice asked.

"What's wrong? Everything's wrong. Clara Andrews is being a complete dictator when it comes to this charity event. I wish we had never voted her chairperson."

Aunt Alice, Carter, and I exchanged looks. I don't think any of us knew what to say to that. I definitely wasn't well-versed in snobby country club politics. I didn't get why Aunt Jeanie always wanted to hang out with these women she couldn't stand.

Aunt Jeanie frowned. "Carter, what are you doing here?"

"Just hanging out," he answered.

Aunt Jeanie looked like she was about to say something, but then shook her head. I didn't think she had the energy. "Okay." Then she sniffed the air. "What is that I smell?"

"Chocolate cake," Aunt Alice answered. "It should be ready soon."

"Alice, are you crazy? I said no sweets!"

"Jeanie, it's just a little weekend treat. It's not that big a deal," Aunt Alice answered.

"Okay, then it won't be that big a deal if I throw it out," Aunt Jeanie said, storming toward the kitchen.

"Jeanie, you better not," Aunt Alice said, following her. I knew a fight was about to take place, and it was not going to be pretty.

Carter took that as his cue to leave, and I couldn't blame him. "I guess I'll see you Monday, Bex. I had a fun day."

"Me too, Carter," I said as I walked him to the door.

On the porch he gave me a fist bump before walking to his car. I watched him drive away before closing the door. It had been a magical day. Carter was so sweet and easy to get along with. I couldn't wait to tell my friends about the wonderful day I'd had. I felt amazing, but I still felt like I was forgetting something.

11

Love and Soccer

—feeling guilty ☹

Dear Love Journal,

Being in love is the best feeling I've ever had. I just hope it doesn't cost me my friends. Really, it was an honest mistake, but they're acting like it's the end of the world.

"So, how'd it go?" Santiago asked as I placed my lunch tray on the table. It was spaghetti day, and I couldn't wait to dig in.

"What?" I asked.

"Decorating the booth," Lily-Rose replied. "How did it go?"

That was when it hit me. The booth was the thing that had been nagging me all Saturday. How was I ever going to explain this to them?

"See, what happened was—"

"Bex! Please don't tell me zat you did not decorate zee booz," Marishca pleaded.

I sighed. I might as well tell them. "Guys, I totally forgot, but I have a really good reason."

Everyone groaned, and I felt incredible guilty. I hated letting people down.

"What? What is the reason?" Chirpy demanded. "Did somebody die?"

"No," I answered quietly.

"Were you sick?" Lily-Rose asked.

"Was there some kind of family emergency?" asked Jeeves.

"No."

"Then what is it? Why didn't you decorate the booth like you promised?" Santiago demanded.

"Because Carter came over," I mumbled under my breath.

"What?" Lily-Rose demanded.

"Because Carter came over," I said a little louder.

Santiago scoffed. "You're joking, right? You blew off the booth for your stupid math tutor? That's not cool, man."

"He's not stupid. I'm sorry, all right?"

"Bex, that was the only chance we had to get the booth decorated," Maverick said. "What are we supposed to do now?"

Chirpy stabbed her spaghetti with her fork. "I'll tell you what we're supposed to do. Have a plain, ugly booth that's not going to attract any customers, and we'll make no money for the leukemia foundation. That burns my biscuits. Thanks a lot, Bex."

"I said I was sorry."

Marishca shook her head. "Sorry doesn't cut it. You let us down."

"I know. I can decorate the booth right before the carnival begins. Don't worry. I'll make it up to you guys, I promise."

They said nothing. I knew they were mad, but I had honestly forgotten. It's wasn't like I'd done it on purpose. "Don't you guys want to know how it went?"

"No!" Everyone yelled at me. Sheesh.

"All right, all right." I had suddenly lost my appetite. It was hard to eat when everyone at your lunch table was mad at you. I figured it would be best if I just left. I slung my bookbag over my shoulders and carried my full tray away from the table. My friends had a right to be mad and my guilt had ruined a perfectly good spaghetti lunch.

"Carter! Pay attention!" Coach Barba yelled.

I had just let a ball get past me and into the goal. After what had happened at lunch, my head just wasn't in the game.

Coach Barba blew the whistle and waved us all in. "The official game season starts next week. We play Evercrest Middle first, so we really need to nail our plays."

This was my first year being on the soccer team, but I knew that Evercrest Middle was our rival and biggest competitor. They had a great team, and being the goalie for our team…that put a lot of pressure on me.

I ran toward the locker room with the rest of the team, but Coach Barba called me back. "Bex, can I talk to you for a second?"

"Yes, Coach Barba?"

"How's math going?"

"It's getting better. I passed my last test with a high C, and that brought my average up. I'll have to get an A on the next one though, but I think I can do it."

"I hope so. We really need you, and you only have two more weeks to bring that score up," Coach Barba said.

I nodded. I already knew that. I was trying my hardest and getting better and better with each tutoring session, but this was a lot of pressure. My whole team was depending on me. I hoped I didn't let them down like I had let my friends down.

12

Ava, Ava, Ava

cringes

Dear Love Journal,

If you ever see me about to make a fool out of myself to impress a boy, please let me know. What happened today was just . . . I don't even know.

Ava showed up to Monday's tutoring session with something covered with pink wrapping paper.

"What's that?" I asked.

"It's a gift for Carter for helping me. I'm doing so much better in math now," Ava answered sweetly.

"Yeah, because you were doing great in the first place," I thought to myself.

"Thanks," Carter said, taking the tray. "Can I open it now?"

"Sure," Ava replied.

Carter ripped off the beautiful paper Ava had wrapped so carefully like a three-year-old would, and I chuckled to myself. Underneath the paper was a tray of heart-shaped brownies wrapped in plastic wrap. I couldn't believe the nerve of this girl.

"They're heart-shaped brownies," Ava announced as if Carter couldn't see.

"Oh," Carter said. "Thanks. I love brownies."

Ava smiled slyly. "I know. Do you know why they're heart-shaped, Carter?" There were lots of things wrong with Ava, but I admired her boldness.

It took every fiber of my being not to kick her.

"N-no," Carter said.

"I think you do, Carter." Ava winked at him.

"Is there something in your eye?" I asked her.

"No."

"Maybe it's one of your fake eyelashes," I suggested.

Ava scowled at me. "I don't have fake eyelashes, you moron!"

"Hey, hey, hey," Carter said. "Let's focus on the lesson."

It was hard to concentrate with Ava staring dreamily at the love of my life and watching him eat her disgusting brownies. I wouldn't have been surprised if she'd laced them with some sort of love powder that would make him fall in love with her. I'd always suspected that Ava was some sort of witch.

When our session was over, Carter packed his things, and I offered to walk him to the door.

"I'll see him out," Ava offered.

"I will. I live here," I said.

"You can both walk me out," Carter said, since Ava was being completely annoying.

Still carrying the tray of brownies, Carter stepped out onto the porch. "Well, see you tomorrow, girls. Thanks again for the brownies, Ava."

"Anytime," Ava replied. "Uh, Carter, may I talk to you for a second?"

"Sure," Carter answered.

Ava glared at me. "Alone."

What did she have to say to him that she couldn't say in front of me? Then Ava stepped onto the porch with Carter and rudely closed the front door in my face.

I knelt and carefully opened the mail slot in the door and pressed my ear against it. I guess I looked pretty stupid, but I had to know what Ava was saying to him.

"So, Carter, I really like you, and I was wondering if you wanted to hang out sometime," Ava said.

There was a brief pause. I felt awkward for the both of them.

"Um, Ava, I don't think that's a good idea."

"Why not?" Ava sounded angry.

"For one, I'm your tutor. Second, I'm too old for you," Carter answered.

Good response, Carter. Better not to tell her about us. It would only make her more upset. I mean, Ava and I were the same age, but I was a clearly a more mature thirteen.

"What?" Ava demanded. "Are you kidding me? You eat my brownies and then say you're too old for me? I'm very mature for my age, you know."

"Ava, I'm sorry. Any boy your age would be lucky to date you, but I just can't," Carter said. "Sorry, I have to go."

"Give me back my brownies!" Ava screamed.

I ran from the door so Ava wouldn't know I'd been listening. I sat at the dining room table and began my homework. It took Ava a moment to come back inside.

She trudged back in with her tray of brownies. I wanted to be happy about her rejection, but I couldn't be. Even though I knew that if it were the other way around she'd be reveling in my sadness.

She placed the tray of brownies on the table and plopped into a chair. "Carter is a loser. He's an awful tutor and I'm not wasting another second on these stupid tutoring sessions."

"If he's so awful why'd you make him brownies?" I asked.

"Shut up, Bex!"

I was beginning to feel as if that were her favorite phrase.

"Ava, I heard what happened out there," I admitted.

For a second Ava looked like she was going to cry, then her sadness turned to anger. "If you tell anyone about this, I swear, I will make your life absolutely miserable!"

Of course, she had a reputation to maintain. Girls like Ava never got turned down by boys. As much as I disliked Ava, I decided that this was something I would keep to myself. She should have known better than to ask

Carter out though. I'd told her that we were going to the carnival together and that Carter had spent Saturday afternoon with me. You would have thought she would have gotten the hint. One good thing did happen as a result of Ava's bold move: she didn't attend any more tutoring sessions, and her math scores miraculously improved overnight.

13

Bex + Math = Okay

—feeling successful ☺

My friends only spent half of the day not talking to me. I had promised them that somehow I would get the booth decorated the day of the carnival and that it would look fantastic. We'd heard through the grapevine that the Avas had hired a design team to do their booth, and my friends thought that our booth needed to be better. I hadn't even seen the Avas' booth, but I didn't think that could happen. And who hires decorators for a carnival booth? Those girls were so lazy!

I was really tempted to tell my friends what had gone down between Ava and Carter, but I'd promised myself that I'd keep it a secret. I knew if I were in Ava's shoes, I wouldn't want the whole school to know that I had gotten rejected.

After school I spotted Ava and Santiago in the almost deserted hallway in front of the auditorium. She had him pinned up against the wall, and almost seemed like she was threatening his life. As I approached, she let him go, and he took off running down the hallway.

"What was that about?" I asked Ava as we both watched Santiago scurry away.

"Keep your nose on your face and out of my business," Ava replied.

"Whatever," I said as I began to walk away, but something pulled me back. Ava had grabbed onto my backpack.

"You should tell your aunt to fire Carter. He's the most horrible tutor ever. She's wasting her money on him."

I sighed. "Ava, just because he turned you down doesn't make him a horrible tutor. It makes him smart. Besides, you should have known better. Carter only has eyes for me."

Ava threw her head back and laughed heartily as if that were the funniest thing she'd ever heard. I wished some of the gunk from the ceiling would fall into her mouth.

"You can laugh all you want, Ava, but you can't win them all, and by all, I mean Carter."

"That jerk is going down," Ava said.

I didn't have time to worry about what she meant because I had to get to soccer practice. Thanks to Carter, it looked like I might actually get to stay on the team. He was my mathematical hero.

I was so glad to have our tutoring sessions back to one-on-one. Learning came so much faster without Ava around to distract me. I had a huge chapter test coming up on Friday that I was a little nervous about. It was a big grade, and if I failed it, no more soccer team for me, and the girls were depending on me. Carter assured me that if I kept practicing, I wouldn't have any problems.

Again I stood in the doorway and watched Carter drive away. I closed the front door and leaned against it like people do in the movies when the love of their lives has just walked out. I couldn't wait for the next day. I lived for these tutoring sessions.

Aunt Jeanie came down the stairs at that moment and interrupted my good thoughts. "Bex, can I ask you a question?"

"Sure, Aunt Jeanie," I answered skeptically. There was no telling what would come out of her mouth.

"How do you feel about Carter?"

I gulped. Did she know? How could she know that Carter and I were in love? I couldn't very well tell her the truth or about our date to the carnival. She'd fire Carter and never let me see him again.

I struggled to think of an appropriate answer. "Uh… "

Aunt Jeanie frowned. "Do you think he's really helping you? I just got off the phone with Mrs. Groves, and she told me that Ava didn't find the sessions very beneficial."

Yeah, because Ava's a lying, manipulating cretin. "Aunt Jeanie, you've seen my last test scores. They've gone up, and I know I couldn't have done it on my own. Carter is definitely helping me. Without him I'd be failing."

Aunt Jeanie nodded. "You're right. Your scores have gone up. I just want to make sure. Are you sure you like Carter because he's helping and not because he's . . . visually appealing?"

So she had noticed. "Is he visually appealing? I guess to some people he might be if you're into that surfer-boy kind of look. I hardly notice what he looks like," I lied.

Aunt Jeanie raised her eyebrow at me. I was now convinced that her one eyebrow was a lie detector. She was about to bust me any second. "Okay," she said finally. "I'm glad he's helping you."

She continued through the living room, and I breathed a sigh of relief. I couldn't believe that Ava was trying to get Carter fired. There was no way in the world I was going to let her ruin this for me.

14

Triangles Are For Geometry Not Pre-Algebra

—feeling confused ☹

Dear Love Journal,

I never imagined that I would be caught in the middle of a love triangle. There was a time when I thought a boy would never like me. Now I have two great guys to choose from. The answer is obvious, but I hate to hurt someone. I never wanted to be the reason someone's heart was broken, but sometimes you just can't help it.

Friday night my friends and I were going to the skating rink. Austin was meeting us there like he did every other

Friday. I really needed this weekend to unwind. That chapter test in Mr. Hawthorne's class had been a killer. I felt okay about it, but I wouldn't find out my score until Monday.

The girls and I were trading our sneakers in for skates at the counter when Austin showed up.

He stood at the entrance of the skating rink looking around for me.

"There he is," Lily-Rose said in my ear. "Austin is the perfect guy for you, and you're willing to toss him to the side for some high-school boy who doesn't even like you in that way."

"Austin is great, and she doesn't deserve him," Marishca added.

I was sick of them giving me grief because of this. I wanted them to mind their own business. I didn't get in the middle of their romantic affairs—most of the time—and I would have appreciated the same courtesy.

Austin spotted us, waved, and ran over. He looked so eager and happy to see me that I felt horrible. I knew what I had to do, and the sooner I did it, the better it would be for everyone.

"Hey, guys," Austin greeted us. He gave us his usual lopsided smile that I'd always liked. His wavy chestnut hair and large brown eyes weren't bad either.

He looked great in his hockey jersey and blue jeans. I could smell the mint gum on his breath.

"Hey, Austin," Chirpy answered. "Remember, no matter what happens, it's not you, it's Bex."

"But don't hold it against her, she's lost her mind," Lily-Rose added.

"Don't you guys have to go find your dates?" I asked, pushing my friends away.

Austin frowned as he watched them skate off. "What was that about?"

I shrugged. "You know my friends, weirdos."

Austin laughed. "Let me get my skates, and then we can hit the rink."

As Austin paid for his skates, the DJ put on a slow song. I watched as everyone paired off skating hand in hand. I noticed each of my friends with their boyfriends skating along happily. I knew that Austin would want to skate with me, and that would just make it worse; I needed to end this now.

"Austin, can we talk over here?" I asked, leading him to a table in the snack area.

"Sure," he said.

As we sat down at the table, my hand touched the sticky surface. I looked at it and grimaced. There was no telling what had given the table that gummy texture.

"Let me get you some napkins," Austin said, standing up.

Why did he have to be so sweet? He was going to make this harder than it already was.

"No, it's okay."

Austin bent down to remove one of his sneakers, then he stopped. "Bex, I'm glad you wanted to talk, because there's something I've been wanting to ask you for a while. I should have asked you a long time ago."

"Austin—"

"I know we've been in this weird place where we're friends but more than friends, and I think we should finally make it official."

"Austin, please—"

"Bex, will you be my girlfriend? Not my friend who's a girl, but my *girlfriend* girlfriend?"

I'd been waiting for a while for Austin to ask me that. A big part of me didn't want him to ask because I didn't think I was ready for that even though the rest of my friends were going out with someone, but a small part of me had always wanted him to ask. I realized a long time had passed and I still hadn't given Austin an answer.

"Well?" he asked.

I knew I was about to hate myself. "Austin, I can't. I'm so sorry. I just don't think it's going to work out between us."

He looked as if I had punched him in the face. "Oh."

"I'm sorry." I kept saying that over and over because I didn't know what else to say.

"I'm confused. I thought you liked me all this time."

"Carter, I did—"

"Carter, who's Carter?"

Nice going, Bex. "What?"

He scowled at me. "You just called me Carter."

"No, I didn't. You just heard me wrong."

Austin narrowed his eyes at me and nodded. "That's why. There's some dude named Carter in the picture. Really, Bex? After all we've been through, you're going to drop me like a hot potato for some loser?"

"He's not a loser. You don't even know him!"

"Ah, so there is a Carter," Austin concluded.

I couldn't lie to him any longer. "Yes. I'm sorry. Maybe if you had asked me to be your girlfriend sooner things would have been different."

"You said you were okay with us just being friends and hanging out for a while. I was okay with that too. So does this *Carter* go to your school?"

"No, he's in high school," I mumbled.

"What?"

"He's in high school," I repeated.

Austin laughed at me. It wasn't his usual nice-boy laugh. It was that jerky kind of laugh.

"What's so funny?" I demanded.

"That's what it is. There's something girls like about older guys. Trust me. A girl like you isn't ready to date some kid in high school."

I felt like he was going out of his way to insult me. "What does that mean?"

"You may look like a high-school girl, but you're not," Austin said.

"Are you using this chair?" asked a girl pointing to the empty chair at our table.

Austin threw his hands up. "Take it. As a matter of fact, you can take this one too." He slipped his foot back into his sneaker and left me sitting at the table alone. I had known that this wasn't going to be an easy conversation, but I hadn't expected it to feel like this. I felt as if someone had dropped a bowling ball on my toe.

After that I didn't feel like skating. I wanted to go home, but I would have to wait for Marishca's mom to pick us up, and that wouldn't be for another hour and a half. I watched my friends skate happily with their dates. I felt like an evil person because while I should have been thinking about how much I had hurt Austin, I was imagining Carter and me skating along hand in hand.

I felt like what I had done to Austin had been so right and so wrong at the same time.

The girls took a break and skated over to the table.

"Where's Austin? Why aren't you guys skating?" Chirpy asked.

"We broke up," I said, although I wasn't sure that was the right terminology since we had never been an official couple.

"Why?" Marishca asked.

"I had to break it off. For Carter."

My three friends moaned.

Lily-Rose rested her forehead on the palm of her hand. "Bex, please tell me you did not break up with a super-cute, super-nice boy who's crazy about you for some crazy crush."

"I really wish you guys would stop talking about our relationship like that."

"Dag nabbit! You are not in a relationship with Carter!" Chirpy shouted.

I scowled at her. I had a few choice words for all of my friends, but I wasn't in the mood to fight with them.

Lily-Rose put her hand on Chirpy's shoulder. "Calm down. We can talk to her until we're blue in the face, but she won't get it. I think we just have to step back and let her learn the hard way."

"Hello, I'm right here," I said. "Stop talking about me like I'm not."

Marishca stood up. "Lily-Rose is right. Let her do what she wants, let's go skate."

I watched my friends glide away across the floor. They were so wrong about Carter and me. Once they saw what a great couple we were, they'd be eating their words.

15

Bex + Big Mouth = Angry Friends

tapes mouth shut

Dear Love Journal,

I feel like a total wicked witch after breaking things off with Austin. I talked to Aunt Alice about it. She told me that it never feels good to break someone's heart, but not wanting to hurt someone's feelings isn't a reason to stay with them. It wouldn't be fair to me or Austin. Aunt Alice says that I did the right thing, but that's only because she doesn't know the full story. I didn't tell her I had dumped Austin for Carter. I guess maybe I was a little ashamed.

I expected my friends to be angry with me on Monday, but thankfully they weren't. I was having a pretty good day considering that it was a Monday. I had received a high B on my chapter test, only a few points from an A. I had even gotten the bonus question correct, and it had been super-difficult. I wouldn't have any problem staying on the soccer team if I kept this up.

At lunch Chirpy was telling everyone at the table about the swim meet she'd had on Sunday. She had come in second place. We were having a decent conversation and congratulating Chirpy until Santiago came to the table.

"So," he said to me, "I hear you let lover-boy go in the middle of the skating rink. That was cold, B."

How did Santiago know anything about that? I shot my friends angry glances. They all gave me that it-wasn't-me look.

"I promise, we didn't say a word about it," Marishca said.

I believed her.

"No," Santiago said. "I heard some boys talking about it at the park yesterday."

I swear. The walls in this town must have ears.

"I don't want to talk about it," I said quietly.

Ava stood at the end of the table. I braced myself. She only stopped by when she wanted to insult one of us, usually me.

"Have any of you seen any flying pigs?"

"What?" Jeeves asked.

"I've seen the day when Bex Carter turned down a perfectly adequate guy who's actually not a loser. Pigs must be flying."

"Get out of here, Ava," I said as I stirred my cafeteria chili. I felt indifferent about the chili. It didn't taste all that great, but I was starving, so it would do for now. Also it gave me something to do other than look at Ava.

"How do you know about that?" Lily-Rose asked.

Ava put her hands on her hips. "Austin told his mother, and his mother told my mother, and then I told everyone. I'm dumbfounded. It's like one of the great mysteries of the world. Trust me, Bex. A girl like you can't afford to go around breaking up with boys who are actually not losers. Only girls like me can do that. Keep it up and you'll end up old and alone or with some tuxedo-wearing freak like Jeeves."

"Hey!" Jeeves cried.

"You can go away now," I said forcefully. This matter was none of her business.

"Fine, but don't say I didn't warn you," Ava said before spinning on her heels and walking away.

I silently made a wish that her father's job would get transferred to Siberia. I could not stand that girl!

"Why did you break up with him?" Maverick asked. I was offended by the fact that he and Lily-Rose were attempting to eat their lunches with one hand because their other hands were intertwined with one another. Couldn't they give it a rest long enough to eat their food?

"He just isn't the one for me," I answered simply. I did not want another fight.

"She dumped him for that Carter dude," Jeeves answered. "I agree with Ava. Big mistake."

"Yeah, well I agree with Ava about you being a tuxedo-wearing freak!" I shot back.

Jeeves looked down at the table, and I immediately wanted to eat my words. "I'm sorry, Jeeves."

Everyone at the table shook their heads and looked down at their food. I was sick of them judging me.

"You're all jealous," I said. A voice in my head was telling me to stop. My nana always told me, once words came out of your mouth, they were out. You can apologize for them all you want, but you'll never be able to undo the hurt they cause. But still, my mouth wouldn't stop.

I looked at Chirpy, Lily-Rose, and Marishca. "You're just mad because I'm going to the carnival with a high-school guy and you're not because you're stuck with middle-school children." Then I moved on to the boys. "And you guys are just jealous of Carter. He has a car, and he's mature, and he could grow a mustache if he wanted to."

Santiago touched his upper lip. "Hey, I could grow a mustache."

"Bex, stop it," Marishca said.

"No. If you guys can't support me and my relationship—"

Chirpy rolled her eyes. "You're not in a relationship!"

"Stop saying that!" I shouted at her. "If you guys can't support me, I'm going to have to ask that you all leave my Awesome-Possum table."

Everyone continued to eat as if they hadn't heard me.

"I mean it. You guys are not allowed to sit at my table anymore," I told my friends.

The bell rang, telling us lunch was over. Everyone stood and gathered their things.

"That's what I thought," I said as I watched them. "And don't come back until you're ready to be real friends," I ordered.

"Whatever, Bex," Lily-Rose muttered. "And we're not jealous. We're just trying to keep you from making a fool out of yourself."

Well I wished they had tried harder, although it probably wouldn't have made a difference.

16

The Intervention

—feeling sad ☹

Dear Love Journal,

I was totally unprepared for what happened today.

Now that I had broken things off with Austin, Carter and I were free to be together. I decided to look extra cute for my tutoring session. I brushed my hair three times. Each time I brushed, new tangles emerged, but my hair looked better than it normally did. I threw on a pair of ripped jeans and a yellow shirt with a glittery smiley face on it. I put on some lip gloss and headed downstairs to wait for Carter.

Aunt Jeanie was gone, and Aunt Alice was busy in the kitchen making a peach cobbler. I went in to see what she was doing.

"Aunt Alice, what's gotten into you?" I asked. She wasn't the type who cooked. I knew for a fact that she ordered take-out every night.

She rolled a pie crust out on the counter. "I don't know. There's something about this kitchen that makes me feel like a domestic diva. My tiny kitchen doesn't motivate me to cook."

Aunt Jeanie lived in a studio apartment. It was small, but it was cute and just right for her.

"Oh, okay," I said, just as the doorbell rang.

I ran to get it. I let Carter in. He was carrying a pink gift bag. "Hey, Bex. This is for you."

I felt like my heart was doing flip-flops in my chest. "What is this?"

"Just a little something for doing so well on your last test. I want you to know how proud I am of you."

"Oh." I took the bag over to the dining room table and looked inside. I pulled out a purple-and-white soccer ball. In the middle was my name. "Carter, thank you so much." I could tell he had put a lot of time and thought into it.

"You're welcome. I'm glad you like it."

"Like it? I love it!" I said, hugging the ball to my chest. I closed my eyes and imagined Carter and me playing soccer together.

"Uh, Bex. It's just a ball," Carter said, laughing as he took a seat.

I shook myself from my daydream. Carter was wrong. It wasn't just a ball. It was a symbol of our undying love.

In the middle of our session, Aunt Alice sat down with us at the dining room table with her laptop. "Don't mind me. I need to type up these recipes before I forget them."

We didn't mind. She typed away, and we continued to work. When our session ended, Carter packed up his things, while I continued to work on the last problems of my homework assignment.

"You know," Carter said. "I've been wondering, they're having a photo exhibit down at the museum. It's on the evolution of photography. I thought maybe it would be cool for us to check it out."

I couldn't believe it. We were already going to the carnival together, and now he was asking me on another date. I looked up to accept his invitation, but something was wrong. He wasn't looking at me. He was looking at Aunt Alice.

She froze, her fingers curved over her keyboard, and looked from me to Carter. "What?"

"Since you're into photography, I thought it would be nice for the two of us to go," Carter explained.

Aunt Alice cleared her throat. "You mean, like a date?"

"Yeah," Carter answered.

"What?" I asked. I felt like someone had just hit me in the chest with a sledgehammer. It took me a few moments to process what was happening. Carter was asking my aunt on a date.

Aunt Alice looked as if she wasn't sure how to respond. "Carter, I'm flattered, but I think you're a little young for me."

"A little young?" I shouted. "He's sixteen and you're ancient!"

"Bex!" Aunt Alice said.

"Carter, what's wrong with you? What about us?" I demanded.

Carter looked at me as if I'd asked him the stupidest question in the world. "Us? What about us?"

"Yeah, us! We're going to the carnival together. You came over and spent that Saturday with me. You winked at me *twice.* You bought me a soccer ball. Do those things mean nothing to you?"

Carter rubbed his forehead. "Aw, man. Bex, I'm sorry. I didn't mean any of those things in *that* way. And I thought I explained about the carnival. I didn't know you were thinking about us in a romantic way." Then he looked at Aunt Alice. "I'm sorry if I read our situation the wrong way."

"What makes you think she would want to go out with a high-school boy? You're just a kid to her," I said. The last sentence caught in my throat. I was just a kid to Carter.

My cheeks burned. I had no idea how red I was, but I must have been pretty red. I wanted to evaporate into thin air. Plenty of bad things had happened to me—I was a walking disaster after all—but nothing that felt like this. I think that was the moment my heart officially broke and I felt guilty for making Austin feel that way. Nana was right. What goes around really comes around.

The three of us sat in awkward silence. Finally Carter stood up. "Maybe I should leave."

"Yeah, maybe you should," I said. All I knew at that moment was that I never wanted to see him again.

He raced toward the door as if the house were on fire. After the door closed, Aunt Alice and I let the silence linger. I couldn't even look at her.

"Bex, I—"

"How could you do that to me, Aunt Alice? I trusted you."

"Honey, I didn't do anything. I didn't know he was going to do that, and I had no idea you had a crush on him."

I slammed my pencil down. No more homework was getting done that night. "It wasn't a crush. I was in love for the first time, and you stole that from me. Thanks a lot." I left the table and stormed toward my bedroom yelling, *"I hate you! I hate you! I hate you!"* Aunt Alice followed behind, but I ignored her.

Just as I reached the staircase, the front door swung open. Aunt Jeanie stepped inside and looked around cautiously. "Hey, what's with all the yelling?"

"Ask your sister. She totally stole my boyfriend!"

"What?" Aunt Jeanie almost dropped the box she was holding.

"Jeanie, it's just a big misunderstanding," Aunt Alice said quietly.

121

I squeezed the banister with all my strength. Maybe that would release some of my anger. "There was no misunderstanding. Aunt Alice wrecked my relationship. Now little Beckham will never exist."

Aunt Jeanie set the box on the floor and closed her eyes. "Listen, I had a rough day. I have no idea what you're talking about, but Alice, whatever it is, you're not leaving here until you fix it. I can't deal with the teenage dramatics tonight."

Aunt Alice threw her hands up as I turned to stomp up the stairs.

"Don't bother," I yelled. "She can't fix this. She totally ruined my life, and there's nothing she can do to change it!"

I slammed my bedroom door and climbed up to my bed. Burying my face in my comforter, I cried my eyes out. I felt sad, broken-hearted, angry, betrayed, and stupid all at the same time. I never wanted to see Aunt Alice or Carter again. They were dead to me.

I cried myself to sleep for about thirty minutes when there was a light tap on the door. I didn't want to talk to anyone, and I wished I had thought to lock my door after slamming it. After I didn't answer, Aunt Jeanie stuck her head in.

"Bex, the girls are here to see you."

After Carter and Aunt Alice, they were the last people I wanted to see. They would only laugh at me and say "I told you so." I didn't need that right now.

"I don't want to see anyone," I said.

"Okay." Aunt Jeanie closed the door. A moment later Marishca, Chirpy, and Lily-Rose entered my bedroom. I'd just said that I didn't want to see anyone. What was wrong with these people?

Marishca closed the door behind them, and the three of them stood there with their arms folded across their chests.

"What are you guys doing here?" I asked.

Lily-Rose spoke first. "Bex, this is an intervention."

I sighed and lay back on the bed. This wasn't the first intervention they'd tried to perform on me. They'd held one when they thought I was addicted to red velvet cupcakes. (You can never have too many red velvet cupcakes.) They had one when I wouldn't stop watching the Arkansas Hacksaw Attack over and over. (Hey, it's only the best horror movie ever made.) The first intervention they held was the time I wouldn't stop wearing overalls in the fifth grade. I thought they were really cute and fashionable, but apparently I was wrong.

"Bex, look at me," Chirpy ordered. She sounded like she meant business, so I sat back up. "This Carter nonsense is going to stop. You're acting like a complete fool, and it's just not acceptable. Don't make us have to banish you from the tribe."

I burst into tears and covered my face with my pillow.

"Nice going, Chirpy," Marishca muttered as they climbed the small ladder to my bed.

"Bex, I was kidding. We'd never banish you," Chirpy said gently.

I felt someone stroking my hair. "It's not that," I said.

"Bex, you wanna take your face out of the pillow so we can hear you?" Lily-Rose asked.

I turned over. My friends looked down at me. "It's not that. It's Carter."

"Oh, what about him?" Marishca asked.

"He doesn't like me. He likes Aunt Alice. He asked her out right in front of me. You guys are right. I'm a stupid fool."

"Aww, Bex, I'm sorry," Chirpy said. "I really am."

I sat up. "I don't get it. If he doesn't like me in that way, why did he agree to go as my date to the carnival?"

My friends looked at each other. Chirpy put her hand on my knee. "Bex, he didn't agree to that."

"Sure he did. I asked, 'Would you like to go to the carnival with me?' He said, 'I'd love to.' You guys were there."

Lily-Rose frowned. "Bex, did you just check out in the middle of that conversation?"

"What?"

"You asked 'Would you like to go to the carnival with me?' He said, 'I'd love to, but that probably wouldn't be a good idea since I'm your tutor and older than you. Besides, I'm already going with a girl from school. I'm sure you'll have fun though.' I remember that word for word because I was so embarrassed for you."

I looked at the other girls. Lily-Rose couldn't have been telling the truth. But Chirpy and Marishca nodded, so I knew that she was. I felt like the biggest idiot ever.

I buried my face in my hands. "Can I just move to Zimbabwe or somewhere very far away and start all over?"

Marishca took my hand away from my face and held it. "Bex, that's why we were so worried about you. You acted like you hadn't even heard Carter, and you were carrying on this imaginary romance in your head, and it was kind of scary."

It all made sense now. Carter taking too long when getting snacks from the kitchen. Carter staying for dinner and baking chocolate cake with Aunt Alice. Carter coming over that Saturday just to hang out. It wasn't for me at all. He'd only wanted to spend more time with Aunt Alice.

The more I thought about it, the more stupid I felt. I couldn't blame Carter. Aunt Alice was beautiful and sweet and fun. What boy wouldn't have a crush on her? If he had turned down a girl like Ava, why would I believe that he would like a girl like me? Stupid, stupid, stupid.

"That's why we didn't understand why you broke things off with Austin, a boy who really liked you," Chirpy said.

The mention of Austin's name made me cry all over again. Lily-Rose lay my head in her lap, and the three of them stroked my thick mane of hair and let me cry. I appreciated them not talking in that moment. I deserved to have my heart broken. I had done the same thing to Austin for no good reason. I had been friends with him for a while, and I just dumped him for golden highlights and dimples.

"I'm a terrible person," I muttered.

"No, you're not," Lily-Rose said forcefully. "You're a great person, Bex. So, you made a mistake. Love makes people do silly things."

"Yeah," Chirpy agreed. "And we're just starting. This time it was you. Next time it'll be another one of us acting crazy, and the rest of us will be there to bail her out. It'll probably be that way through high school, college, until we get married."

I laughed, but that seemed like an awful long time. My heart hurt so bad I couldn't see myself loving anyone else. I wasn't sure I wanted to.

At that moment I was extremely grateful for my friends. They had said a lot of things that had hurt my feelings, but they were only looking out for me. I figured it wasn't a coincidence that a girl like me who did so many stupid things had been blessed with such smart friends.

17

Carnival of Horrors

—feeling worried ☹

Dear Love Journal,
   Love stinks. That is all.

At long last the time for the dreaded carnival rolled around. I wasn't looking forward to it for several reasons. For one thing, it reminded me of how I had let my friends down when I'd forgotten to decorate our booth because I was hanging out with what's-his-face. That's what I called him now. Saying his name was too painful. Now I hated the fact that his name was also my last name. I couldn't get away from that.

Secondly, all my friends had dates to the carnival except for me. I didn't have a job to perform at our fortune-telling booth because I had planned on spending the entire night with what's-his-face.

Anyways, my friends were super-troopers. They arrived two hours before the carnival began to help me set up.

We'd hung a sign that read "Fortunes" and decorated with all the stars and moons I'd made the day before, and it looked pretty good. I thought if I were visiting a carnival that the booth would make me want to stop and get my fortune read.

Once we were done decorating our booth, I decided to take a stroll and see what the other kids had come up with. Most of them had created some kind of game where you could win a stuffed-animal prize—bean bag tosses, dart throwing—typical carnival games. Ours was the only fortune-telling booth.

I passed the Avas' booth—as pink and purple as it could be. It did look very professionally decorated with cut-outs of lip-gloss tubes and powder compacts. I couldn't help but to roll my eyes at their sign: "We can make you look ALMOST as beautiful as us."

Ava T. and Ava M. were setting things up. Ava G. was nowhere to be seen. Of course she would leave all the hard work for her loyal followers.

As the sun began to set, people entered the carnival grounds. It was showtime.

Marishca looked great as she sat at the table with her crystal ball. She had a purple scarf tied around her head while she wore a large white blouse and a long, flowing blue skirt. Lily-Rose sat with a stack of cards she'd purchased from a gift store, and Chirpy was ready to read palms. Jeeves stood in front of our booth trying to draw customers in. "Come one, come all. Come get your fortunes told by the one and only Madame Marishca. Find out what destiny has in store for you."

A man and his wife stopped by the booth. The man sat at the chair across from Marishca. I stood nearby because I wanted to see how Marishca planned to pull this off.

She closed her eyes and waved her hands over the crystal ball she had found at a thrift shop for three bucks. "Oh," she said, nodding. "I see somezing."

"What?" the man asked eagerly.

"You and your wife are expecting a baby."

"Yeah," the man said.

"The baby will be a boy. He will be a bright, happy, healzy child. He will play baseball."

"Wow. Yes, we are having a boy," the man said, sounding amazed.

Marishca told him some more wonderful things about his life, and then Santiago shooed him away when his two minutes were up. "Another five bucks if you want to hear more."

The kid was a shark.

"Marishca, how on earth did you know all that stuff?" I asked her.

"Easy. His wife was wearing one of zose Lenora bracelets. She has the charm with zee teddy bear wearing a blue bowtie. That means she's having a boy. My aunt has zee same one. The man was wearing a baseball jersey, so I assumed he was a baseball fan. The rest was just general stuff."

Soon a small line began to form. I was excited about that until I saw Carter toward the end of the line. He was chatting with some girl who I assumed to be Heather. Just seeing him made my stomach hurt. Without saying anything to anyone, I slipped away. I decided to explore the carnival on my own.

I took a ride in the haunted house on my own. It was lamer than usual. Really, who would be afraid of orange glow-in-the-dark spiders? During the ride I thought about how Austin and I would have spent the whole time making fun of it. After that I bought myself a funnel cake to snack on while I decided what to do next.

"Where's your date, Bex?" a familiar voice asked.

I turned to see Ava sitting alone on a bench, which was unusual for her. She was usually surrounded by hordes of adoring fans. Also she was wearing blue jeans and a gray hoodie, which was *very* unusual for her. I'd never seen Ava dress that way.

"He went to the bathroom," I lied.

Ava called my bluff. "Liar. I saw him walking around here with that other girl."

I sighed and sat next to Ava with my funnel cake.

"I told you," She continued. "The guy's a jerk."

I didn't know whether Carter was a jerk or not. For a while I'd hated him, but it was my fault my heart had been broken. I'd seen what I wanted to see and made a big deal out of nothing.

"I don't know," I said. "He's right. We are too young for him."

"Bex, my father is twenty years older than my mom," Ava said.

"I think when you get older it's not that big of a deal, but now it is."

Ava pulled the hood over her head. "Anyways, that creep is going to get what's coming to him. I think you'll be very happy by the end of the night, Bex."

"What do you mean?"

"Remember the day you saw me talking to Santiago in the hallway?"

The day she'd had him pinned against the wall and he'd looked like he feared for his life. "Yeah."

"I was hiring his bodyguard services. Tonight two of his guys are going to beat Carter up."

"What? Ava, are you crazy?"

She looked at me. "Bex, nobody crosses Ava Groves. Not even some stupid high-school boy. What's wrong with you? You should be thanking me. This will be payback for both of us."

"No way, Ava. I want nothing to do with this." I stood, leaving my funnel cake on the bench. I had to get to Santiago and make him call this off.

Ava grabbed my arm. "Bex, don't you dare mess this up. I paid good money for this beat down."

I yanked my arm away from her and kept walking. Just when I thought she couldn't get any more evil, she had gone and proved me wrong.

Back at our booth, I spotted Santiago shoving a stack of money in his pocket after collecting money from a customer. I pulled him away from the booth.

"Hey, I'm busy here," he complained.

"Santiago, did you or did you not let Ava hire two of your bodyguards to beat Carter up?" I demanded.

Santiago looked around and adjusted the collar of his shirt. "Yeah, I did, but that's confidential."

"Santiago, are you crazy? How could you do that? Your guys are supposed to protect kids from bullies, not beat up innocent kids."

He sighed. "I know, I know. I didn't really want to do it, but Ava—she paid me a lot of money, and she's really scary, Bex."

"Santiago, call it off right now," I said.

"Bex, do you know how much she gave me?"

"Now, Santiago!" I shouted.

"All right, all right, but her deposit is nonrefundable," he muttered. He took out his cell phone and pressed a button. The phone on the other end rang and rang. "No one's answering."

"Leave a message."

"Hey, Luis. Listen, the job is off. I repeat, the job is off," Santiago said. He hung up and sent a text.

I felt terrible. I had no way of knowing whether or not Luis would get the message in time. "Where is this supposed to happen, Santiago?"

"Whenever they find Carter in a deserted area, in the bathroom, wherever."

"So they're just following him around?" That was super creepy. "Santiago, you're going to come and help me find him."

"I can't. I have to collect the money," he said.

"Let one of the others do it. Come on."

We went by the booth and told Maverick that he needed to take the money from customers and then we went to find Carter.

"Oh, Ava is going to kill me," Santiago whined.

"You let me worry about Ava," I told him.

We must have circled the carnival twice, weaving in and out of people, making sure not to step on discarded snow cones or old pizza crusts. I finally spotted Carter waiting in line for the Double Loop roller coaster. He had his arm around Heather. They were talking and looking very happy. That sick feeling rose in my stomach again.

Santiago and I pushed our way through the line.

"Hey, no cuts!" somebody yelled, but we ignored them.

It wasn't until we reached Carter that I realized how ridiculous this story was going to sound.

"Carter," I called.

He turned and looked surprised to see me. "Oh, hey, Bex."

We stood in an awkward silence for a few moments. This was the first time I had seen him since the day he'd broken my heart.

"Umm, Bex, this is—"

"Yeah, yeah, Heather, I know," I said. "Listen, I know this is going to sound crazy, but you have to get out of here."

He looked at me suspiciously. "Yeah, why's that?"

"Because two guys are planning to beat you up," I answered.

Carter bit his bottom lip. He looked so cute when he did that. *Focus, Bex.*

"Right. So I suppose I should leave the carnival."

I shrugged. "I would. These are big dudes, Carter. Not your average eighth graders."

Carter patted me on the head like a puppy. "Nice try, Bex. I think I'll be all right."

"Look, man, she's serious," said Santiago. "I know because they work for me. Ava Groves hired them to beat you up because you made her mad. I'm telling you man, making that girl angry is not a smart move."

Carter looked back and forth between Santiago and me. "Seriously? That girl has some issues."

"Yes, she does," I agreed.

"You know what's weird?" Carter asked. "That fortune teller told me I was going to have bad luck tonight."

"Don't worry," Santiago said. "For the low price of twenty dollars I can offer you bodyguard protection—"

"Santiago!" I yelled. "Carter, what are you going to do?"

"Don't worry, Bex. Now that I know I'll keep my eyes peeled for them, and I'll stay in the open. I'll be okay. Thanks for the heads-up, though." Then it was his and Heather's turn to board the ride.

Santiago and I ducked underneath the rope to get out of the line. I heard a dinging in Santiago's pocket. He removed the phone. "The guys were waiting by Carter's car in the parking lot, but they got the message. It's off."

I nodded. "Good. Thanks, Santiago."

"No prob. And Bex, that guy's not all that. You can do much better," he said, patting me on the shoulder. "I'm going to get back to the booth. If you see Ava, tell her I moved to Mexico."

I looked back at the Double Loop and envisioned Carter and Heather riding, holding hands, squishing together in fear. I suddenly didn't want to be at the carnival anymore. I just wanted to go home.

18

Making Up

—feeling relieved ☺

My Aunt Jeanie didn't like to waste any time. On Monday afternoon she already had a new tutor lined up for me. His name was Natesh, and his mother was a member at the country club.

I can assure you that I would not be developing a crush on this tutor. It's not that Natesh was all that bad— okay, he was. He smelled like cheese, and he wasn't as nice as Carter. He was super smart and explained things well, so I figured he would get the job done.

Later that evening as I did homework on my bed, someone knocked on the door.

"Come in!" I called.

The door opened slowly, and Aunt Alice peeked in. I knew we were long overdue for a conversation.

"Can we talk?" she asked.

I closed my science book. "Sure."

She climbed the ladder that led to my bed and sat on the edge of it. I hadn't said much to Aunt Alice since that dreaded day with Carter. I had realized a while ago that none of this was her fault, but I didn't know what to say to make things between us better, so I'd said nothing. I had said some terrible things to her that she would never forget.

"Aunt Alice—"

"Bex—" We spoke at the same time.

"You first," Aunt Alice said.

"I'm so sorry. I had no right to get mad at you and say the horrible things I said. You didn't deserve that."

She pushed my hair behind my ear. "What happened?"

"I really, really liked Carter, and I kind of lost my mind I guess."

Aunt Alice frowned. "You let a boy come between us?"

I guess I had. My friends and I had promised that we would never let that happen to us, and here I was, doing it to my own aunt. What kind of person was I?

"Bex, what have I always told you? When it comes to guys, keep your cool. You should never try to impress a boy. Let them impress you."

She had always told me that. "I did stupid things, Aunt Alice. I let my friends down. I watched him at the wave pool. I argued with Ava over him."

"Bex, fighting over a guy is so lame," Aunt Alice said.

She wasn't making me feel any better, but she was saying what I needed to hear.

"When a boy likes you, you won't have to fight for him."

"I broke up with Austin for him. He'll never speak to me again."

Aunt Alice smiled at me warmly. "You won't know unless you try. Give him a call and see what happens."

"Love is so stupid."

"No, it's not, Bex. I know it seems that way sometimes, but it's the best feeling in the world when you find the right one. I haven't yet, but I know I will. You, my dear, have a long way to go, so take it easy. Don't rush it."

I didn't think I could take a lifetime of this. Ever since Carter had asked Aunt Alice out, I'd felt like a cloud was always hanging over me that would never go away.

Aunt Alice put her arm around me. "Don't fall in love so fast."

She gave me a squeeze and then hopped down from the bed.

"Aunt Alice?"

"Yeah?"

"You're not ancient and I don't hate you. I'm sorry for all the mean things I said."

She blew me a kiss. "I forgive you—this time."

I smiled as she closed the door behind her. I had a lot of thinking to do.

Sunday evening I went by Austin's house. He wasn't expecting me, but I had some things that I had to get off my chest.

I rang his doorbell and sat on the porch. A moment later the door opened and closed. I looked down at my lap. I didn't think I could look Austin in the eye after the way I'd treated him. I felt him sit beside me.

"What's up?" he asked.

I wasn't sure what to say. I didn't know what I expected from him. I was happy he was at least talking to me.

"I just wanted to apologize. I shouldn't have tossed you to the side like that. You're a great guy, and you didn't deserve that."

"Thanks," he answered. "You hurt me, Bex. I thought we had something special, but I guess heartbreak is a part of life. I guess I'll get over it eventually."

There was a long pause. I watched a man cross the street with his little twin boys.

"So," Austin said. "What's up with you and Carter?"

"Nothing. Absolutely nothing."

"So that's why you're here?"

Finally, I looked at him. "No, that's not why I'm here. I wanted to apologize. I don't want you to hate me."

"I don't hate you," he said quietly.

"Do you think we can be the way we were?"

He shrugged. "Right now I think we should just be friends, which we kind of were before. I don't know if I'm ready for the girlfriend thing right now."

I nodded in agreement. "Yeah. I need to focus on math and our new soccer season. My heart has had enough for right now."

Austin took my hand and squeezed it. "Friends?"

"Yeah," I answered. It wasn't exactly what I wanted. I wanted to be half of a couple like my other friends, but love wasn't something that could be forced. You just had to let it happen, and that's what I planned to do. Focus on Bex, and when love happens, it happens.

Austin and I sat silently on the porch for a long time watching the cars pass. I had a feeling that one day Austin would change his mind about us, and when he did, the timing would be perfect.

Life lesson from Bex: Never lose your head over a guy. Just be cool.

Keep Reading for a sneak peek of *Bex Carter 3: Winter Blunderland*

Other books in the Bex Carter Series:
#1 Aunt Jeanie's Revenge (now available)
#3 Winter Blunderland (now available)
#4 The Great War of Lincoln Middle (Dec 2013)
#5 TBA (Jan 2014)

Join the list to be notified of new releases:
http://eepurl.com/HappH

An Excerpt from Bex Carter 3: Winter Blunderland

When I got to the rec room, Jade was already standing outside with her hands shoved in her pockets. "Hey," she said. "The boys are already out back."

"Out back?"

"Yeah, out back behind the rec room. It's where we hang." We watched several kids go into the rec room. "It's where the cool kids hang out," Jade added.

I was excited. I had no idea what we were going to do, and I loved the mystery of it. My excitement quickly faded when I realized that "out back" meant away from the light. Liam and Mason were in the dark woods waiting for us. Almost every horror movie I'd ever seen started off that way.

As we approached the boys, I was happy to see they were at least carrying flashlights. I also smelled something that smelled like . . . cigarette smoke.

"Hey, Bex," Liam said.

"Hey."

"Glad you could make it," Mason said.

I nodded. "Me too. What's that smell?"

Liam sniffed the air. "Oh, that. I don't know. Someone must have been out here before us."

I guessed that was possible.

Jade took Mason's hand. "Should we tell her now?" Mason asked.

"Yeah," Jade answered. "She's cool."

"Have you ever heard of the ghost of Treetop Villas?" Liam asked.

Just the mention of the word "ghost" made me shiver. Even with the flashlights, the woods were still eerie. "No."

"Of course not. You've never been here before." Liam put the flashlight underneath his chin to give himself that creepy storytelling look. I'd done that with my friends plenty of times when I told them ghost stories, but it was much scarier in the woods at night.

"Wh-what about the ghost?" I stammered, trying not to sound afraid, but it wasn't working.

"We've been coming here since we were kids," Liam continued. "Around the time we were ten, five years ago, strange things started happening around the villas. Strange knocks on the windows at night. Wailing heard from the forest. Strange footprints on people's porches. People started saying that a ghost haunted the Villas, and it kind of became a legend."

Just as he said that, a gust of wind blew through the trees. Even though I was halfway to being scared out of my mind, I was a sucker for a good ghost story. "What's the legend?"

Mason cleared his throat. "This ski lodge is built on an ancient burial ground."

Seriously? How unoriginal.

"One of the people buried here was a man named Old Man Murray. He was the meanest, grumpiest old man who ever lived. Even when he was alive, he hated for anyone to come on his property. So you can imagine how he felt when they decided to build Treetop Villas on his final resting place. He was furious. It's said that when this place was first built, each winter someone mysteriously disappeared. They even shut the ski lodge down for a few years. We've seen copies of the police report. It's true."

Another gust of wind caused me to shiver.

Mason dropped his voice so I had to lean in closer to hear him. "One winter the people who owned the lodge hired a ghost hunter. He did whatever it is that ghost hunters do and caught Old Man Murray's spirit."

So much for details.

Mason continued. "So anyway, everything was peaceful and there were no signs of Old Man Murray until several years ago. That's when the strange things we mentioned earlier started happening again."

38426494R00090

Made in the USA
Middletown, DE
19 December 2016